"Oh, Tess. Don  pass."

Leah's drawl is so thick the statement sounds like a sampler embroidered on a pillow in her grandmother's South Carolina parlor.

"Yeah, it might pass like a kidney stone, but it will pass." Carrie laughs and picks up her phone, taps a button, and repeats the phrase. Yup, she records what she considers clever quotes. I wonder if she's planning a career in stand-up or plotting a tell-all memoir. Both are possibilities with her, and each scare me equally.

"Geez, Care, the joke wasn't that funny." Mel waves her hands in the air. "If you want a good one, try this—Life is not a fairy tale. If you lose your shoe at midnight, you're a sloppy drunk."

"Heard that one before," Alexa says.

"How about an Adam roast?" Rory asks. "We should stop calling him your Ex. We should call him your Y. Like why did you date him?"

The Roast

by

Ally Hayes

The Roast

Cover Art by *Jennifer Greeff*

The Wild Rose Press, Inc.
PO Box 708
Adams Basin, NY 14410-0708
Visit us at www.thewildrosepress.com

Publishing History
First Edition, 2021
Trade Paperback ISBN 978-1-5092-3870-5
Digital ISBN 978-1-5092-3871-2

Published in the United States of America

Dedication

To my girlfriends
old, new, near and far

Chapter One

I thought I knew pain. Sure, turning down Adam's proposal hurt, but the pain felt like a quick sting compared to the incessant stabbing I feel today.

Today is his wedding day. Not mine.

I'll be fine. I got this. *Snort.* I can't even kid myself. Thankfully, my friends don't believe me either. They'll be here soon. I don't know what they concocted for tonight, but I'm certain booze will be to blame tomorrow.

By now I should have accepted the reality. Adam has been engaged to Brittany for roughly six months. Sure, not a ton of time by traditional standards, but enough time to absorb the news. My goal was to be copacetic by today. I thought I could convince myself to be strong, but strong does not describe my present state. My only comfort is knowing I'm not the only one who can't let go.

Late last night my cell phone came to life. Not that I was asleep, but I still startled. From my nightstand, the photo linked to Adam's contact card shone in the darkness. He leaned against the hood of his old pickup truck, gazing off in the distance. I remember the day I snapped the picture like it was yesterday, not nine years ago while I was still in high school. I had silenced the device earlier, but curiosity prevented me from shutting down completely. As it vibrated and blinked, I darted out my hand on instinct. Clenching the device to my chest, I felt my heart race. I resisted answering right away, hoping to catch my breath. I ended my self-inflicted torture with a tap of the green button, selected the speaker option, and kept my voice cool. "Hello?" Not a casual "hey," or "what's up?" No, last night was not for light banter or false impressions.

"Tess?"

I could barely hear his usually strong, confident voice. The frog in my throat prevented me from answering his greeting.

"Am I making a mistake?" he asked.

I hit the Pause button on my tablet. Silly cat videos could wait. "Oh no, you don't! You can't lay that one on me." I straightened from my slouched position against my headboard and tightened the elastic that slipped loose from my long, straight hair.

"Yeah. I know, not fair."

"But," I hesitated just a beat to search for the right words. I resisted the temptation to yell. "If you're having doubts…" I could picture his muscular shoulders slumped forward and him hanging his head. His big, coffee-colored eyes squinted in thought or were even closed as he sometimes did during painful situations.

"Not doubts, exactly."

A muffling sound filtered through my phone's speaker. Several more followed.

"I'm just thinking. Like, you know?"

Irritated by the breathing sounds, I snapped. "No, Adam, actually I don't know." I hated sounding mean, but whenever I think of Adam and Brittany together my stomach tightens, and I spew vicious words. I sweated from head to toe and kicked off my sheets.

"Hey! Remember, you said no."

"I remember." I flushed again from the roots of my hair to my bare feet. My body temperature rivaled the August heat which proved no match for the weak air conditioning unit blasting from my bedroom window. Massachusetts might be known for long winters, but late summer in the city can rival any southern state. Wearing only a tank top and worn-out pajama shorts, I had nothing left to strip to cool off.

I heard no response from his end. Finally, a faint sniffle.

"Would you still say no?"

My stomach lurched and I doubled over, attempting to quell the roller-coaster sensation before responding. "I don't know." I didn't intend to sound sheepish, but my response came out in a whisper.

After I delivered the cruel words, a wave of nausea rose as if by punishment. I felt selfish and childish, yet I refrained from whining. I desperately wanted to beg Adam to call off the wedding. By then I was too late, though. Several times I blew my opportunity to make a rational argument. I never pursued it, because naively, I believed this day would never arrive. Their engagement wounded me, but I never told him. Maybe I could have prevented this union. I'll never know because I remained stoic, hoping to call his bluff. Now, my stubbornness and pride got me nowhere as he will approach the altar in a few hours due to his own.

Hearing his voice last night, the meek version, hurt deeply as I wondered if that phone conversation would be our last. Instead of professing my undying love, I bit my lip to keep from speaking my heart as I should have

3

when I had the chance months ago.

We ended the call with pathetic apologies, a half-hearted wish of good luck from me and a weak mumble of thanks from Adam. With trembling hands, I powered down my phone for the night. I never surrender the possibility of contact on normal nights. Last night was not normal, and I highly doubt tonight will resemble anything close to normalcy.

I woke early this morning, jolting upright with the immediate awareness of the Big Day. Okay, maybe I never slept last night. My sheets were a tangled mess after hours of fitful tossing and turning. Now, at noon, I'm punchy. I repeatedly clench and release my hands. I scan the apartment for an area I might have missed to clean.

Maybe I should have accepted my roommate's offer. Before she left, Alexa repeatedly asked if I'd be okay spending the morning alone if she went to the gym. Hovering at the door, she asked for the last time.

I walked toward her, waving my bottle of all-purpose cleaner in the air. "I'll be fine, go ahead."

"Sweating could be cathartic."

"I'm sure it would, but no thanks. Don't worry about me. I won't do anything dumb." I sensed she needed to get away from me for a bit, especially while preparing to support me tonight. Even I know I'm sure to be a handful.

"Okay. Well, if you're sure." Alexa pushed her light brown, bob into a headband. She swiped her water bottle and keys from the entryway table and slipped out the door without another word.

In lieu of a workout, I turned to my favorite coping mechanism—cleaning. Now, as my first guest arrives,

I'm wiping the kitchen counters for the third time. I already scrubbed and vacuumed all morning to calm my nerves. The smell of disinfectant still hangs fresh in the air, and I swear the scent slows my racing heart. While annoying to some, for me it's aromatherapy.

The unlocked door to my apartment opens slowly with a steady creak. My best friend, Mel, peeks her head into the room just far enough for me to spy her blonde, springy curls.

She holds a recognizable white paper sack and offers a too-big, fake smile. "I have your favorite! Wait, are you alone? You shouldn't be alone, and you should coat your stomach before you start drinking." She glances around the room, spinning in a circle. "You haven't started yet, Tess, have you?"

"Somehow, I resisted." I plop on my couch and motion for her to join me. Her mere presence immediately calms me. Finally, I relax my hands. "I chose my other addiction, bleach."

Mel sniffs the air. With a curt nod, she deposits the bag on my coffee table and creates placemats out of the deli wrap. The crinkling ceases, and Mel places a napkin to the left of my sub and cracks open the bottle of water before me.

I assume she has an agenda; she always does, and today would not be the day to start living like a pantser. I fold my hands and await further instructions.

"I guess obsessive cleaning is better than drinking alone. I think you should put away the chemicals and prepare for the festivities though. Now, have a couple of bites then tell me two reasons why you are too good for Adam."

My best friend is pushy in all the right ways.

Nodding, I snap off my rubber gloves I forgot I still wore. They are practically a second skin. A grumble from my stomach reminds me I haven't eaten yet today. This morning, even the mere thought of my usual black coffee made me want to barf. Now, carbs might be a welcome addition in my empty gut. As if on cue, it rumbles again. I lift half of my sub and obey Mel's command by cramming two large bites of my favorite combination of turkey and Muenster cheese into my mouth. The tangy mustard tingles my nose.

I deliberately chew extra slowly to buy time to concoct my reply. After a loud swallow, I dab the corners of my mouth with the stiff napkin and turn to Mel. I hold up the thumb on my right hand. "One—I have a brain." I extend my pointer to join my thumb. "Two—he doesn't."

Mel rolls her eyes. "That's a start. Not a good one, but you'll get there." She pats my back.

Her touch feels reassuring. Over the years, she's calmed me countless times. From skinned knees and bad grades, to boys and job interviews, Mel was always there for me. We've been friends since meeting on the playground in first grade.

"Hi, I'm Melissa Ruggerio, and don't you dare ever call me Missy." She hoisted herself onto the swing next to mine.

I was thrilled this girl with the leopard-patterned leggings chose to speak to me, but I wanted to look cool, so I continued pumping my legs and gazed straight ahead. "Okay, Mel."

She didn't hop off and join the group of girls gathered at the slide as I feared.

I breathed a sigh of relief.

While sharing an after-school snack with my mom, I announced my triumph. "I made a new friend today."

"Oh?" She raised an eyebrow and lowered her carrot stick.

"Yup. Mel Ruggerio." I dunked my celery in the cup of dill dip on the table between us.

"Sounds like a tough name for a little girl. We'll have to watch out for her."

Mom was wrong. Mel is a marshmallow, and as for watching out, Mel is practically my guardian angel. The idea of her being tough, though, intrigued me, and I brought her a candy bar the next day. We've been inseparable ever since.

I place my sandwich down and tap the home button on my phone to illuminate the clock. The afternoon is wearing, and I see flashes of wedding preparations. Try as I might, I fail to prevent the slideshow in my head. Each virtual slide causes bile to rise and burn in my throat.

"Ugh, she's probably getting her hair and make-up done right now. I had to find a nail salon seven miles away yesterday for fear I'd run into her." I display my coral manicure, still pristine courtesy of the gloves.

Mel flips my phone face down and scoots it out of reach. "If you think I will tolerate you checking your phone all night you are sorely mistaken. In fact, when everyone gets here you should probably shut it off." She cocks her head to the side. "I'll allow one exception. Did you already talk to your parents?"

I nod. I normally text or talk briefly with my dad every day. Nothing major. We just check in with each other and exchange funny videos, like pals. That's how we roll. My relationship with my mom is good now but wasn't always. Since childhood, I've been closer with my dad who supported my whims. With no other siblings to resort to, he encouraged everything, including baseball and hockey. My mom trod carefully around me while my dad played cheerleader. I know now she feared sabotaging her one shot at parenting and felt like she held her breath until I grew up. After my volatile teenage years, she and I became closer and found a good place to confide and share. I tested those boundaries this week.

"The usual with my dad. He steered the conversations toward the Red Sox and my job to play it safe. My mom texted every morning with some words of wisdom she must have pulled from an inspirational self-help book or page-a-day calendar. She called each night, and I swear just to ensure I didn't sound like ending it all before she could deliver another quote the next morning. Today, she called three times. During the last conversation, I lied and told her Rory had just walked in the door, and we were about to bake a cake."

Mel's eyes widen. "And she believed you?"

I shrug. "I doubt it, but she sounded satisfied to hear about Rory. Sorry, but if I said your name, she would've revved her sedan and beelined over."

She smiles and waves her hands. "I guess I can't blame her. With my checkered past and all."

Mel has repeatedly assured me she doesn't mind her reputation as a bad influence because she knows the truth. She gets a kick out of my mom believing Mel is behind all my bad decisions. Conversely, her parents think I'm an angel, and I'm more than happy to let them.

After a quick glance at her phone's notifications,

Mel rises and paces the room. "This new?" She selects a blue striped pillow and punches the perfectly fluffed square. After muttering about a sale online and repositioning my pillow on the couch, she turns away and walks toward the kitchen.

Judging from the bend of her head and arms, I suspect she is sneaking another peek at her phone. I hear the faint tapping of fingernails as if she is typing with her phone set to silent.

Mel's voice from the other room cuts the silence. "Let's watch something mindless until the others arrive." She returns to the room and picks up the TV remote, selecting the on-demand menu. She scrolls through the titles of sitcoms and finally settles on an episode I've seen a million times.

While I wonder what Mel's phone alerted her and imagine all sorts of catastrophic scenarios, I choke down half my sandwich while watching the fictional family spar about money. Soon, I hear the apartment door squeak open again.

Alexa reappears freshly showered and even dressed and made-up for the evening. Further evidence to support my suspicion she needed ample distance from the time bomb I'm sure to become. She joins us on the couch without a word as if afraid to disturb the peace.

She keeps her gaze fixed on the TV.

I can't tell if she's paying attention, but I have nothing to say anyhow. At least nothing nice, or positive. I pretend to follow the on-screen dialog while I recall declarations of undying love Adam and I exchanged over the years. The other two also stare blankly at the TV, and I wonder if they are lost in thought as well. Other than my attempts to stifle a few sniffs, I remain silent for another half an hour.

The credits roll on the screen and above the encore of the theme song I hear a faint knock on my door.

Mel and Alexa rise from the couch.

Leah and Carrie saunter in together, followed by Rory. They all carry shopping bags and cases of beer. They stall in the narrow foyer.

Only Rory leans in for a quick hug. She pulls back and pushes a stray hair off my cheek. "You okay?"

I nod and offer a tight smile.

Rory was my college roommate who now lives with Mel in an apartment a few blocks away. Leah and Carrie share a duplex a little farther out of the city and are the only set of our friends to have an actual yard. The space barely accommodates two Adirondack chairs, but I would kill for their patch of grass.

I met Leah and Carrie on the first day of seventh grade. My elementary school merged with theirs in the town's small junior high school. The unlikely duo already shared best friend status before I met them. Carrie towered over Leah even back then. Leah's southern accent clashed perfectly with Carrie's attempts to sound like she hailed from the inner city and not our small western suburb. I pointed out the girls to Mel, and I was relieved she found them as impressive as I did. I was attracted like a magnet and recruited Mel to follow Leah and Carrie through the halls and laugh at everything they said. Hero-worship equals friendship in seventh grade. By mid-year, I was considered their friend. Years later, I considered them family. Today, they are like vital organs.

Mel rises from the couch and takes a bag from Carrie's hand and a twelve-pack from Leah. "Let's get to work." She turns to me and shakes her pointer finger back and forth. "You stay right here, and don't look at your phone."

I make a cross over my heart. "Yes, ma'am."

They arrange my apartment in what can only be described as a mock-bachelorette party. From my perch on the couch, I hear the rustling of plastic bags, slamming of cabinets and drawers, and the beep of my oven timer. I don't hear chatter and become nervous. Our group is a lot of things, but quiet isn't one of them. I defy Mel's order and tiptoe toward the kitchen.

The tiny kitchen peninsula separating the rooms is now a makeshift bar, and the card table Alexa and I use as a dining table displays old photos of us. Bowls filled with my favorite chips and candy dot the end table next to the couch. On the coffee table sits a lone box of tissues. A fitting centerpiece.

God, I love these girls. I rise from the couch and inch closer to the kitchen. "Can I do anything?"

Leah approaches, shaking her head.

The motion causes her hair to bounce like a model's in a shampoo commercial. Her perfect beach waves have somehow defied the ninety percent humidity level of this late summer day. Kudos to whatever product she is paying big bucks for lately.

She twists off the top of my favorite brand of light beer with a hiss and extends the bottle. "G'head." She taps her own amber bottle to mine and parts her lips to take a swig.

"Not yet! I heard a clink." Mel shouts from the kitchen. "Wait for the rest of us. You'll know when we're ready."

Carrie enters the room, clutching a red plastic cup.

She licks her fingers.

"Do I smell fried chicken?" I'm only humoring her. Of course, it's fried chicken. Can anything else match that salty, oily aroma? Carrie's mom must have been cooking early this morning. "Your mom is a saint, Carrie."

"She didn't want us going to the bars hungry. Consider it her contribution." Carrie cackles. "The black contribution."

She is always pointing out her race. I let it go. It's her personal thing, like Mel's baby blonde hair, Rory's ever-preppy clothing style, or Leah's deep southern accent she can't shake despite living in Massachusetts since she was ten years old.

"Hey," Mel yells, hands on hips and now pointing at Carrie. "My mom sent lasagna and garlic bread. There's room for more than one cultural stereotype in this group."

True, we represent a motley group. I'm a mutt of sorts nationality-wise, but the girls like to say when I drink beer or whisky, I get my "Irish up." I don't think they mean I speak with a brogue.

Unlike most groups of girls, we do not have a redhead. I started the joke about missing a "Jessie" and whenever any of us see a pretty redhead when we're out drinking, I debate approaching her. If a redhead named Jessica in her late twenties is ever listed as missing, consider us prime suspects in her disappearance.

Ignoring my earlier instruction, I drain my beer and pick at the mushy label disintegrating from the condensation. Picking keeps my hands busy and the nerves somewhat under control. Soon, I hold a pile of sticky mush. Despite the window unit blowing at full speed, the room is still stuffy. I have not ventured out of my apartment today but did see the forecast predicting dense humidity, and I secretly hope it's wreaking havoc on Brittany's thick, wavy hair. I gather my own thin hair into a ponytail and then shake it out, repeatedly.

I wasn't sure how I wanted to look tonight or what vibe I wanted to present. I ransacked my closet and drawers for an outfit making me look put together, as opposed to falling apart, like I feel inside. After many wardrobe deliberations, I selected my go-to skinny jeans, new wedge sandals, and a flowy top paired with a long necklace. If I was just going out on a regular night, and hoping to attract attention, the top would've been six inches shorter. But nothing about tonight is regular. My hair is another issue—pulled back tight means business, loose looks slutty. I'm still debating and fiddling with my stray locks when my friends approach en masse.

All the girls settle into the couch except for Rory.

Rory places her hand on the small of my back and nudges me toward the center of the room. "It's time."

Grateful for the one beer headstart, I nod and approach my square wooden coffee table. A thrift store find now boasting water rings the size of beer bottles and coffee cups. I slip off my sandals and hop up on what has become our group's stage. Usually, I take this stance to dance, sing, or lead my friends in a drinking game. Not tonight.

"First, thank you all for coming to my, um, whatever this is." I stretch my arms out wide. "Now, let's get some things straight before I'm completely at your mercy. Tonight is all about me. Whatever I want to drink—get it for me. Whatever I want to say—let me say it. If I want to cry—don't stop me. And, of course, someone please hold my hair or give me a scrunchie should I puke." I raise my hand to indicate I'm not finished, and a plastic shot glass is deposited into my empty hand. I down the fireball like a required medicine rendered by a nurse in a clinic. "I just need to survive the night. Let me Adam-bash, mourn, whatever you want to call it, and it will end tonight. I will never make you listen to me gush or hate on him ever again. Even better, do this for me tonight, and I promise if, when, I ever do get married, you'll all get to pick out your own designer bridesmaid dresses and be exempt from all showers."

Carrie stands and leads everyone in a slow clap.

Mel scoots out of sight for a split second and returns with shot glasses for all on a plastic platter.

The content is clear, so I steel myself for any number of poisons. I hope it's something sweet, but it looks like vodka. Vodka this early could be bad. Then again, how could today get any worse? I take the tiny glass and sniff and relax my pursed lips.

"To Tess, we're all here for you tonight." Rory holds her glass up high.

Then everyone follows suit before making history of their first shot of the night.

To my relief, my second shot is Sambuca. She brought the good stuff. The shot goes down easily with a light burn of licorice. I smile and cling to this temporary feeling of content.

An ear-piercing screech interrupts the moment.

Alexa removes her thumb and forefinger from her lips. "Okay, who's first?"

I'm confused and intrigued. I mean, I know they

have something planned, but I don't even have a vague idea of the agenda. I suddenly crave the comfort of my bed and wish I could dash down the hall and dive under the covers. No, that's not true. I want to rewind to yesterday when I still had a chance of preventing this reality. If I knew yesterday how I would feel today, I might have answered him honestly instead of acting tough. I sigh. There's no way to turn back time. The shit-show is underway.

"Me! I'm first!" Leah raises a hand. She points at me then to the couch.

I step down and plop onto the threadbare sectional. The hand-me-down is courtesy of my parents' basement. The rest of the furniture, like the coffee table, was purchased from thrift stores or left from the previous renter.

Leah takes my place on the table. She adjusts her micro-short skirt, flips her hair, and flashes her wide smile. "Do y'all remember the first words Adam said to Tess?"

Ugh, we're leading off with the remember-game. This will get ugly.

No use denying this one, so I play along. "I sure do. He said, 'nice tits.' " I throw back my head and laugh to let them know I'm game. I get it now. My cheeks burn which is appropriate as I realize tonight, I'm being roasted.

Chapter Two

Everyone laughs, except Rory.

She throws her hands in the air. "I'm lost."

"I never told you about our first conversation?" I ask through snorts.

Leah rises from the couch. The laughter slows as she steps onto the coffee table. "Oh, Lord. Let's start at the beginning. For a long time, I thought Tess and Adam met on the highway, because that's where most accidents occur."

Laughter halts.

Leah scowls and puts her hands on her hips. "But really, like any good story, or country song, the story of Tess's obsession with Adam begins in a small town..." She sweeps both arms behind her and bows. She steps down and motions for me to reclaim the coffee table stage. She offers a high five.

I smack her hand, imitating the sub-out pass from junior high school volleyball games. Leah and I swapped spots as setters since we were both only five feet tall. She still is, but I managed to reach five-five by the time I turned seventeen.

Inspired by Leah's introduction, I continue with her theme. I clear my throat and deliberately off-key, sing the first line of a familiar song about life in a small town. The groans escalate, and I hold up a hand to stop them. "Just kidding. It's way too early for this voice.

But, stay tuned." I take another swig and force a burp for dramatic effect and because frankly, I'm a pretty good belcher. "Our town is small…"

"How small is it?"

I grin. Thanks to me, half the girls know classic comedy bits. I take pride in hearing the appropriate response and crave their enthusiasm, so I tip my beer bottle in thanks to the participants before continuing. "Our town is so small we don't have a town drunk, so we all take turns."

Several grunts and one groan.

I feel a smirk tighten my cheeks. Our hometown is small. Not crazy backwoods, inbred-family small, but smallish. Everyone vaguely knows everyone. The two elementary schools feed into a junior high school, so by the time I entered seventh grade, I knew practically every kid my age.

In that hellish institution of social injustice, I first saw Adam. I was a lowly seventh grader, a peon to his god-like status as an eighth grader. The mere sight of him in the hallway caused me to blush and sweat all over. But, like any tween girl vying for a boy's attention, I acted obnoxiously. I flaunted my denim miniskirt and baby T-shirt as if I had the body to fill it out and cruised by his locker several times a day, even though I had no classes in the vicinity. Giggling with my friends behind the safety of my three-ring binders, I avoided eye contact.

The charade went on for months. I drove Mel crazy talking incessantly about his cool, now I know, fake, bad-boy image. I suppose his tough façade led me to assume the precocious, bad-girl look. I recall the effort I put in each day and realize everyone must have seen right through. I laugh now at my naïveté.

"Remember, Tess, you never did actually speak in person that year," Mel says.

"Right, but in my head, I had hundreds of conversations with him in which I was always ready with snappy one-liners and flirty comebacks." I did encounter him in the spring as my homeroom filed into the auditorium for a school-wide, mandatory presentation about the dangers of drugs. Knowing I'd pass right by him, I strutted my stuff. I recently turned thirteen and wore a real bra, with maybe just a little too much padding. As I followed my classmates down the slope to our row, my Adam radar spotted him seated on an aisle. I was thrilled and smiling until I heard the now-infamous first words. I was so mortified I froze in place and stared.

He didn't say another word once I spun to face him.

But his friends laughed hysterically. They called me by my new nickname for the remainder of the year.

Adam did not, at least not to my face.

I clung to that silver lining.

The next fall, Adam went on to high school.

I never saw him, but I continued drawing bubbly hearts with his name on my folders and notebooks all through eighth grade. I experimented with eyeliner and adopted a signature scent, as suggested by teen magazines, while I counted down the days until I could join the real party a block away at Thurston High School.

What would become of us began the summer before I entered ninth grade. Sounds skanky now, but there it is.

"Wait!" Mel climbs up on the table.

I make room and worry for the stability of the coffee table. I wonder if I have enough wood glue left over from a kitchen drawer disaster following a wild night two years ago.

Mel drapes her arm heavily over my shoulder and almost knocks me over.

"The real beginning of Adam and Tess was my fault." Mel hangs her head, chin to chest. But, above her head, she holds an empty shot glass.

Leah hands me a blue, glass bottle of tequila.

I pour a splash in the cup on Mel's head and take a small swig from the bottle and hand it back to Leah.

Mel nods, knocks back the shot, and looks up with a grin. "Guilty. I dragged Tess to the pool one hot, sticky day. She didn't want to go, but I knew Adam would be there. I didn't inform her of that tidbit though. I was having a boring summer and felt like stirring up shit." Mel shrugs and steps down.

Not everyone in the room knows the truth, but I've heard this confession before. I have thanked and cursed her for the devious plan many times over the years.

"Mel's right. I didn't want to go to our town's public pool. I had bad childhood memories of bratty kids peeing in the shallow end and the sting of chlorine in my eyes, but Mel was relentless. She won me over by telling me how great I looked in my new neon-pink bikini."

"Well, you did," she says now.

"Yeah, I finally had something to fill the tiny triangle cups."

"Why a cruddy pool full of little kids then, and not a beach?" Rory asks.

"Again, my fault. I had been tasked with taking my little sister to swim lessons at the pool every afternoon. I knew Adam worked in the concession stand."

I waggle my finger at Mel. "Lest we not forget, you were crushing on Ryan all summer. He worked there, too, so this set-up was as much for you as it was a friendly gesture for me."

Mel's mom dropped us off at the entrance gate. Whenever she left us somewhere alone, she usually told us to have fun, but that day she switched to, "Be good." Mom-intuition is real. I caught sight of Adam at the concession stand window, and I stopped in my tracks. I sucked in my non-existent gut and stuck out my new chest. Sure enough, it worked. As I swaggered by, I heard whistling from the shed. I learned enough from watching teen sit-coms to know to keep walking and suppress the urge to turn my head.

I claimed two empty lounge chairs and set out our matching striped towels while Mel walked her little sister to the lesson. When she returned, I acted cool and chatty and waited an excruciating fifteen minutes before announcing I desperately needed a diet soda.

With determination, I approached the shack slowly, teetering in my platform flip-flops. While standing in line I silently rehearsed my flirty greeting.

The person in front of me stepped aside.

Quickly, I plastered on a wide smile and prepared to address my crush.

Ryan wiped the counter with a rag. His gaze was fixed on a chocolate spot. "What can I get you?"

I dropped my jaw. I totally forgot my smooth opening and struggled to remember to order a drink.

Ryan lifted his head and smiled. "Hey, wait.

You're Tess, right?"

Startled he knew my real name, I felt my cheeks burn. Encouraged, I delivered a line I'd heard in a movie, "The one and only." I tossed my hair behind my shoulders. This move was not intentional, but the bad habit seemed appropriate at the time.

"Right. Well, he'd kill me for saying this, but Adam thinks you're cute. He'd wait on you, but he's shy and ran off to the freezer." He laughed.

I wondered at whose expense.

"I'm not shy, you jerk!" Adam announced with a muffled voice. His head and shoulders were buried in the freezer chest. Adam emerged and handed a push pop to a little girl at the other window then turned to Ryan. "Maybe I'm just not interested."

Although sweating from the neck down, I wanted to sound icy. "Good, neither am I. Can I just have a diet soda?" I waved my dollar bill through the window.

Adam retreated behind a display of chips and pretzels.

Ryan handed over the can of soda with a shrug.

I left the money on the counter and walked away feeling gazes upon me.

Mel lowered her magazine. "How'd that go?"

I cracked open the cold soda can and smiled. "Not bad."

An hour later, Mel left to pick up her sister from her lesson and take her to the picnic area. She was gone for a while, giving her sister a break and snack before letting her join her little friends at the splash pad.

Alone and feeling awkward, I chose a fashion magazine from my bag. I silently answered a quiz on optimum skirt length until I sensed a shadow cover my legs. I looked for the source.

Adam stood at the foot of the lounge chair.

We both wore sunglasses, so neither had an advantage, but mine were saucers behind the shield.

"Look, Ryan shouldn't have said that. I've never told him anything." He sighed and pointed to a nearby empty chair. "Okay if I sit? I'm on break and need to grab some rays. Don't read into it."

I gestured to the chair as if to say, It's all yours, and fought to contain a squeal. I pretended to read my magazine for the next fifteen minutes, side-eyeing Adam behind the security of my sunglasses. I was desperate for him to notice me but couldn't think of anything to say or do without making a fool of myself. I picked my straw bag off the ground and rummaged through pretending I had a mission. I did not, but then spied the coconut-scented, dark tanning oil I swiped from my mother's bathroom. I made a scene of squirting and slowly rubbing the oil onto my legs. Thinking back, I'm sure now I must have looked like I was copying a cheesy music video, but I felt in command at the time. I didn't dare look in his direction during my performance. While applying the oil to my chest, though, I heard his chair creak.

Adam stood between our chairs and cleared his throat.

I snapped to attention.

"So, do you like wanna party tonight?" He kept his gaze off in the distance.

Later, I would know that look like the back of my hand.

I swallowed hard and tried my hardest to sound casual. "Sure, I guess." My pulse raced, and I felt relieved he wasn't looking at me for fear he'd see the sweat forming at my hairline. I also took the opportunity to check out his bare chest.

"Cool. So, just meet at the end of Elm around eight. Bring your friend. Ryan is actually the shy one." He disappeared.

I shrieked all afternoon and convinced Mel we'd have fun. I plotted our outfits and orchestrated lies to our parents. We settled on the old standby of telling them we were spending the night at each other's houses. We were still good girls back then, and they had no reason to doubt us or cross check our stories. My mother would soon discover this trick, and I learned the torture of revoked phone and TV privileges.

After I stashed my pretend sleepover bag in the bushes on the side of my house, I met Mel a few blocks from where Adam indicated. The sky darkened, and the temperature dropped. I hugged my arms around my middle for warmth and to quell my twitching hands. Cicadas screeched, and for once, I welcomed their annoying noise because their racket drowned the sound of my heart hammering away.

Mel chatted incessantly as she tends to when nervous, but I couldn't find my voice. We caught up with Adam and Ryan who were surrounded by other guys I didn't know but recognized.

Adam walked toward me. "Hey," but said nothing more. He hooked his thumbs into the front pockets of his ripped jeans and gave me a quick head-to-toe once-over. He nodded.

I hoped that meant he approved, but I still worried I didn't look mature. My heart raced, and my stomach somersaulted. I tightened my arms around myself.

Mel turned to Ryan. "Whose house are we going to?"

The boys laughed collectively and sauntered down the middle of the street.

Mel and I followed them to the dead end where the woods began. The sky darkened completely while I wove my way through the oaks and pines. Dead leaves and twigs crunched beneath my feet. I feared tripping. I didn't panic until I saw a clearing and the empty beer cans scattered around a bonfire. The realization of being in the woods, with beer and boys, scared and exhilarated me at the same time.

Rap music thumped from an old-school boom box. The boys chugged and shot-gunned cans of bargain beer.

I never asked for one, but when handed a can of beer I accepted by popping the top. I remember being nauseated upon the first sip and laugh now looking at the empties strewn about my apartment. Granted, I've upgraded my caliber of alcohol since the days of drinking in the woods.

I shake my head now. "Beer was so gross back then. I wonder what happens between then and age twenty to our taste buds? Do they give in or give up?"

Leah nods. "Something like that. Same with coffee. A universal mystery."

"Continue," Alexa urges.

She wasn't my close friend back then. Alexa spent her entire summers from ages eight to sixteen at a sleepaway camp. First as a camper, later as a counselor, and those facts represent all the information she's ever shared. Apparently, what happens at camp stays at camp despite my many attempts at getting her to divulge any details.

I faked taking sips of the beer and spilled out as much as I could without notice. A necessary and lifelong skill was learned that night. On the sly, I twisted off the pop-top and pocketed it for posterity. Only one other girl showed up. Tyler's on-again, off-again girlfriend who I would later have a strange relationship with, our friendship dependent on my status with Adam and hers with Tyler as if I could never be her friend on my own. I have no tolerance for fickle friends and lost track of her over the years.

The couple disappeared into the darkness.

I felt Adam's hand on mine. I will never forget experiencing a buzz of electricity and later the fear of never recapturing the sensation.

He led me deeper into the woods. He barely muttered three words, but I didn't care. He was Adam, and he smelled musky. The night was too dark for him to see I was scared, so I let him kiss me and no more. I was very conscious that pushing away his curious hands would make him come back for more, and I was right. Thank God for angsty, young adult books to teach me the not-so-hard-to-get rules.

At eleven, Ryan's older brother arrived in his compact, yet somehow obnoxiously loud, car. The six of us piled in, and I finagled my way onto Adam's lap. At my request, Mel and I were dropped a few houses down from my own. I didn't expect a kiss, but I wondered how Adam would say good-bye in front of his friends. I worried he wouldn't say anything. I was practically out of the car when I heard him clear his throat.

"See ya," was all he said, but those two words had

me floating on air as I ran to my backyard pulling Mel by the hand. I yanked her to the ground with me to crawl past the windows and sneak in slowly through the bulkhead doors leading to my basement. Once inside, I kept the lights off and told her to keep her voice low.

Mel confessed she got too scared to be alone with Ryan.

I exaggerated my escapade with Adam. I was too keyed up to sleep and called Leah and Carrie in the middle of the night to relay the events.

Mel walked home the next morning.

I snuck around to my own front door and rang the bell, as if returning from her house.

My mom met me in the doorway holding a mug of coffee. "Good morning, honey!"

"Hi, Mom." I yawned.

"Oh those sleepovers, I don't know why anyone calls them that. No one ever gets any sleep. Go lie down on the couch, and I'll call you when the pancakes are ready."

"And so began our devious ways," Mel adds now.

Needless to say, I became a regular at the pool. I enjoyed watching Adam's dark hair lighten while his tan deepened. I combated freckles and attempted highlighting my brown hair to no avail with lemon juice. I couldn't talk to him while he worked, but I'd sneak glances and catch him looking, which felt even better than talking. We held hands in the park, kissed in the woods, and by late July we were talking on the phone every night and gone to the movie theater twice. In my book, we were going out, dating—whatever it was called even though I never dared to call our situation anything. Except, Adam asked me to keep us a secret. I know—red flag. I get that now.

I stupidly anticipated becoming a freshman and envisioned high school to be the penultimate event of my life. I felt nervous, but mostly excited to be seen with Adam. However, the first day of school did not live up to my high expectations.

Adam wouldn't acknowledge me in front of his sophomore friends. If he saw me approaching, he turned his back.

By the end of the first week though, I did get a note written by him.

Adam passed the note to Ryan who gave it to Mel who gave it to me.

The note said he'd had fun, but I had to stop chasing him. Total dick move, right? Except he signed it, "Luv, Adam." I should've known then—we were both screwed.

Chapter Three

"Well, you know what they say about a queen without her king?" Leah scans the room.

No one chimes in, and my friends all turn to face me, as if I know what the hell she is getting at, but I'm not about to let my friends down and believe I'm not their queen. "No, what's a queen without her king?" I mimic Leah's accent.

After shooting me a scowl, Leah puts her hands on her hips and cranes her neck. "Historically speaking, more powerful!"

Carrie lets out a snort and follows it with a cackle. "Tell it, girl!"

I probably was stronger without him back then, but of course after he ditched me, I felt crushed. He popped the bubble containing my fantasy of our perfect high school relationship. Gone were my dreams of holding hands in the hallway and stealing kisses by our lockers. I felt like a fool, and I could easily feel the same now without my friends here. I wouldn't have blamed them if they wanted nothing to do with me tonight. They've supported me so many times in the past, I should be surprised they're here at all, never mind indulging me. Thinking about the alternative makes my eyes sting, a precursor to tears for me. I inhale deeply and force a smile while conjuring up a diversion question.

The tears remain at bay for now, so I change the

subject. "What time should we plan to head out?" I fan my eyes and plop back down on the couch.

Alexa extends a cold bottle of water.

I should mention here, she's the smart one. I crack open the top and gulp.

She takes the empty. "You know, Tess, we could just stay in and avoid unknown stimuli. The decision is yours. You shouldn't feel obligated to be social."

She sounds sincere, and I suspect a little worried. I already considered the option of avoiding the outside world. Years of practice have taught me I'm better amongst my people and off my couch where thoughts go dark at night. "No, let's stick with our original plan. I'd like to leave around seven. By then, the reception should be underway. I should get to celebrate, too." I air quote the word celebrate.

Rory looks at her phone. "It's only four-thirty now."

I wince. Time is so cruel—drags during work and workouts, flies during vacations and fun outings. Today is creeping at a snail's pace. I wanted the time to be much later for daring to ask the following question, but I'm impatient. "Have you heard from her?"

"No." Rory looks up, her lips forming a straight line. "Look, Tess, I told her not to call or text. I forbade her, so don't beg me to contact her. I discussed with the girls and decided it's best if you don't know what's happening there."

"I know anyway." I wave the air as if I don't care. "I suppose I don't need Hannah to livestream the details."

One of us is missing tonight. Hannah has a front row seat to the Adam and Brittany show. She and Ryan have been dating seriously for the past five years and living together for almost three. They'll be the next to get married. Their wedding will be interesting to say the least. One of my best friends marrying Adam's best friend. Adam will likely be a groomsman, leaving Brittany to sit with the rest of us. Picturing the scene now, I realize I need to encourage Hannah to elope. Note to self to set up a Go Fund Me as soon as Ryan pops the question.

Originally, Mel planned to attend the wedding too. She was asked by one of the groomsmen, a cousin of Brittany's. By the time she discovered Derek's relation to Brittany, they'd been dating for three months. Another month passed before she informed me about the connection and subsequent invitation. I could only laugh. I am grateful Mel is with me tonight and like to believe she would've chosen me anyway, but loyalty was not the deciding factor. A few weeks ago, Mel discovered Derek's frequent trips to Texas were not for business, but to visit his other girlfriend and their four-month-old daughter. Mel subtracted the 'plus one' from her invitation.

Of course, the girls and I gave Mel a night to remember too after the startling discovery. Hers was more vicious than mine is turning out to be. Mel displayed no tears, only pure rage. I encouraged her to vent. Time and mean tweets have helped her heal.

Great, now I'm thinking about Brittany. "She's probably arriving at the church right now. A photographer is already there posing Adam and his groomsmen at the altar. She's in the white limousine with her parents waiting for her photo op, reapplying her already perfect lipstick." I choke on the last few words. I can practically smell the day lilies in her bouquet, and my chest constricts. Revolting.

Mel grabs my hand and slaps lightly. "Tess, stop. No tears now." She turns to face the rest of the girls and points at Rory. "Sounds like it's time for another shot and a roast."

"Yes, m'lady." Rory skips into the kitchen.

She returns with various shots on an unfamiliar tray.

"Thanks, Rory. I'll take the story from here since you weren't there," Mel says.

"Where?" Rory asks.

"Where this is going, dummy. Just hand me the tray." Mel passes out the shots.

Now I see the white, plastic tray must have been purchased specifically for tonight. The word *Slay* is emblazoned in glittery letters across the center. I hope it's also a hostess gift. I am still the hostess, right? Roastee? "And just where is this going? Besides to Hell?" I ask.

Mel gets in my face and grins. She spins on her heels to face the girls. "Who remembers junior prom?"

Three hands shoot toward the ceiling.

I lift my glass high. "Not me!" The syrupy, sweet shot slides down my throat and numbs the memory forever fresh in my mind, despite the same peach liquor I drank that night.

Our high school, though small, held two proms. A less-formal version in the gym for juniors and a larger, more elaborate deal for the seniors a week later at an upscale city hotel. I thought I'd hit the prom-jackpot since I was dating a senior during my junior year. *Silly teenager.*

"Wait." Rory sets her chin. "When did you get back together?"

"Right, you don't know the timeline. The summer I was sixteen. Almost immediately after I got my driver's license and my grandmother's faded brown sedan."

"Oh my God, remember?" Alexa shakes her head.

"I hope you all do. You guys benefited from the boat-on-wheels as much as I did." I obtained my freedom the same time my parents decided Lois should lose hers. My new independence and set of wheels led me back into Adam's good graces. During my freshman year, he did a stellar job of ignoring me and making me feel invisible. I rallied eventually and concentrated on my schoolwork, sports, and friends. I truly believe if I continued to date Adam, I wouldn't have become close with Mel, Leah, Carrie, Alexa, and Hannah. So, I am now grateful for the reprieve though the delivery stung, okay—killed, at the time. I received exactly three late-night phone calls over the months, but I also answered numerous hang-ups. I knew I still had a hold on him, and I grew to like the situation. During the summer after my freshman year, we hooked up twice, and I thought we'd stay together, but I miscalculated by a year.

On June eighteenth, a day after finishing tenth grade, I pulled my granny-car into the gravel parking lot of the town pool. Despite many attempts to mask the aroma, the plush interior still smelled of wintergreen from both the candy Lois was known for and the multiple air fresheners I removed from the rearview mirror. I was grateful though. Even driving a grandma-mobile beat getting dropped off by my mom or riding my bike. Those days were behind me, and I felt like a badass.

Leah and Mel accompanied me sporting giant sunglasses and see-thru cover-ups. I assured each of them we looked hot.

Personally, I was looking for trouble. I briefly dated two guys since my first kiss with Adam, and I felt ready for a challenge.

Adam had been promoted to lifeguard and was very deserving of the tight red trunks and tank top. He looked to me like he spent the winter in the weight room at school or at one of the new gyms popping up in old warehouse spaces. As my crew and I sashayed past him, I could sense his gaze following me. In hopes of driving Adam crazy, I selected lounge chairs directly across from his perch.

While making out in my car later, he admitted I succeeded.

A week later, I considered us an actual couple. My new status as an incoming Junior and driver justified this Senior publicly dating me.

"Actually," Carrie says, "When school started, he only acknowledged hooking up with you once over the summer. I was there, in his math class, when he told his friends. What a dumb ass. I mean I was in dumb-math for a Junior and he was a year older. It might have even been his second try." Carrie shakes her head and takes a sip of her "punch" through a bendy straw.

She never gave in to beer and drinks rum or gin mixed with any colorful juice exclusively. *Nasty*. I hold my tongue about the dumb reference since I knew why he struggled in math. The year prior was a tough one for his family. I learned the information later, and discovered it was also the reason Adam avoided me. I was touched to discover family comes first to him.

"Correction. He only denied them being a couple at first," Leah says. "He was testing the other guys' reactions. Remember, I was kind of seeing Tommy on the sly early in the year, so I had inside info. The other guys pretty much treated Adam as their leader that year so none of them dared tease him. I think Tess and Adam were considered legit by mid-September because that's when the rest of us junior girls were deemed acceptable to date."

Recalling the power shift, I nod. "Sounds right. I remember all of us enjoying 'cool' status for a few months. We were invited to popular-kid parties, got rides home in muscle cars, and the all-important acknowledgement, 'hey,' from senior boys in the hall. Things were good for a while, but with us, the good times never lasted long."

"Dum, dum, dum. Enter, prom night." Carrie sing-songs.

Adam agreed to take me to my Junior Prom, but with a catch—of course. I was not going to his Senior Prom. He promised to take Gina, who was a close friend of Ryan's and Tyler's dates who were all also Seniors. I agreed, because I knew compromising would be the only way he would go to mine, and because I liked Gina. More importantly, I trusted her. Gina's long-term boyfriend was two years older and in the military. He was currently deployed, so he could not attend her prom. As a sophomore, she went to his senior prom, but not attending your own prom is different. I should know.

I turn to Rory. "So, Adam and I were in a good place during the spring, and I was thrilled to pick out an expensive, yet cheap-looking, dress and ridiculous strappy shoes, and obsess over the details of the perfect night ahead. Ha!"

Leah, Carrie, Mel, Hannah, and I gathered at my house to squeeze into our strapless dresses and flat-iron each other's hair. Alexa was at a salon having her hair and nails done courtesy of her grandmother, and I was jealous.

My mom popped her head into my bedroom a few times despite my earlier warning to keep her distance. Once I was made-up, hair-sprayed, and stuffed into my dress, I welcomed her back by announcing we were ready for our close-ups.

I tilt my head toward my high school crew. "Your dates all arrived fumbling with their florist boxes and tugging at their cummerbunds. You giggled and blushed while you attempted to pin on their boutonnieres and accepted your wrist corsages. You all did a stellar job of not looking at the clock as much as I did." I still remember the nervous sweat and the powdery scent of my deodorant kicking in while the time ticked away. The roots of my hair are damp even now as I recall the humiliation I tried to conceal a decade ago.

"I really thought he'd show," Leah admits now.

"Me too," Alexa says.

"Nope, not me. At five-thirty, I knew disaster was ahead." Mel cringes. "Sorry."

We look to Carrie for her recollection. "What? Oh, I don't know. I was all caught up in myself. Remember? My mom came over to take pictures and was more than a little surprised to discover Kevin was white."

I point and look down my nose. "Well, maybe if you hadn't been referring to him as Key-van for a month she would've had a clue."

Carrie cackles at the memory. Prom wasn't the last time she misled her mother.

Leah doubles over in her chair, snort-laughing.

"What are you laughing at, Leah?" Carrie narrows her eyes.

I wonder if she'll bring up the elephant I've sensed lumbering around the room. I believe the roommates are hiding something I've suspected.

"Nothing." Leah snaps upright then jumps to her feet. She offers to get another round of drinks.

Alexa shakes her almost-empty bottle.

Leah nods and hurries toward the kitchen. She's avoided the subject for now, and I save her by returning to my painful recounting of prom night. "I don't know at what point I knew. I think I held out hope until the last second." I take a swig of my beer just as my throat constricts, causing a choke-cough. "God, those pictures are pathetic. All of you arm-in-arm with your dates and single me on the end like a photo-bomber."

"You looked great." Mel walks over to the table of framed photos. "At least you got this one of just us girls." She brings the photo over.

I smile, glad my mom insisted on making the boys sit one out and arranged us on our back porch. I was nervous, but not hopeless at that point, so my smile was genuine. I thought we all looked fabulous. Jewel tones were the popular color for dresses, and a few of us bore matching orange glows courtesy of the spray tans we splurged on at a sketchy new place. Six months earlier the space was home to my favorite sub shop, but I wasn't deterred from disrobing and getting doused with chemicals where I once ate lunch. Vanity prevailed. Despite the tint and burnt-plastic odor, I thought my friends and I looked like royalty. Little did I know my Prince Charming was about to pull a Cinderella on me.

"So," Rory says. "What happened? Did he call?"

"No." I called Adam's house three times. I listened to incessant ringing but hung up each time the answering machine picked up, convinced the lack of response signaled he was on his way. Back then, he didn't have a cell phone. My flip model was still a novelty and worked virtually nowhere. I held out my last ounce of hope and joined Hannah and her date in their limo. They waited until the last minute with me. The crowd dwindled to just the three of us and my parents standing in my front yard.

My mom paced the sidewalk. She was practically in tears one minute, then full of rage the next.

She was never Adam's biggest fan anyway. She offered to drive me, but I couldn't bear the ten-minute monologue and opted for the humiliation of arriving alone with another couple as their third wheel.

"Car trouble," Hannah explained to a group exiting the limo behind us.

They pointed and spoke behind their hands.

Thankfully, most people stared at Hannah. They always do, and that night no one could look away. Hannah rocked the only mermaid-style dress at the junior prom, and everyone would attempt to copy her look the next year. She was that girl. Still is.

At the door, I presented my two tickets to the guidance counselor who smiled and listened as I explained Adam would be arriving any second. I forget now which line I fed her—car trouble, missing bow tie from the rental place, or wrong shoes. I was babbling. It didn't matter.

She nodded sympathetically and said I looked beautiful. She knew.

After half an hour of lame excuses and the previously mentioned lies to my classmates, I gave in to tears in the bathroom. Too embarrassed to even find Mel, I called my dad from the hall payphone. I hid by the exit, avoiding everyone. Minutes that felt like an eternity later, my dad pulled his car right up to the gym entrance and opened the passenger door for me. He simply patted my hand, and I lost any composure I had left. The only words spoken were his as he ordered us two large, cookie dough cones at the dairy drive-in.

I ignored the ringing from the kitchen wall phone all night. I don't know how my parents tolerated the noise downstairs. My mom removed the pink cordless from my room before I returned home, and I pried loose the battery from my flip. I wrote stupid poems, listened to sappy music, and threw a few stuffed animals at the wall before watching the sun rise and finally passing out upside down on top of my bed.

"Tess."

My mom's quiet, but firm, voice from the doorway woke me the next morning.

"Adam is at the door, and I'm not letting him inside."

I bolted upright and smoothed my hair and dress. Yup, I never took the damn thing off. I rushed toward her. "No, wait! I want to hear what he has to say. Just give me two minutes. I swear! Maybe something horrible happened."

"Tess…" She crossed her arms over her chest and blocked the door.

She stood like a night club bouncer. If bouncers looked like petite, middle-aged women wearing pink monogrammed cardigans.

"I know, Mom." I sat again on my bed, defeated. I sat there for hours. Feelings of rejection turned to rage then back to curiosity with a tinge of longing.

"I'm the one who found the note," Alexa says. "I came over around lunchtime and saw the notebook paper sticking out of your mailbox."

"Right." I nod. "You didn't let my mom know, but he clearly chose his words as if she might intercept." I'll never forget:

Tess, I'll totally understand if you never forgive me. I deserve you not speaking to me right now. I ruined your night, I know. Please believe me when I say I'm sorry, and I swear to you I tried, I really did. I was only 15 minutes late to the gym, but they wouldn't let me in. I could blame the guys, but I'm the one who should take all the blame and punishment. You know where I am when you feel like talking to me. Love, Adam

I read between the lines. He must have been drinking with his friends, and when he finally showed up at the school gym, he was denied entry. Zero tolerance was a new and heavily enforced policy. I was a mess of mixed emotions. Mad and sad battled while I re-read his words.

Thankfully, Alexa swiped the note, crumpled it, and threw it across the room.

Part of me wanted to defend Adam and blame his friends, and the other part hated him for choosing them first.

Alexa called him every swear word she knew back then. While not as vast an arsenal as she has now, she still impressed me.

"Hey, it was easier to help you be mad." She shrugs now.

Leah and Mel came over later, and I ordered pizza, since fitting into skin-tight dresses was no longer a concern. Baggy sweats and oversized T-shirts were the outfits of choice. I offered snacks and movies to avoid any prom talk.

They slept over and not until Sunday morning did they dare ask me my game plan.

"Hear me out," I said.

I remember Alexa raised one eyebrow and shook her head but kept silent.

"I'll forgive him if he takes me to his prom."

Alexa crossed her arms over her chest. "Nope. I'm out. I can't support this one. You're on your own."

"For the record, I don't like it." Leah shook her head. "Basically, he chose to get sloppy with his senior friends instead of being there for you."

"I'm with her, but I know my vote won't make a difference," Mel added.

I laughed. "You're right, it won't. I do my own thing despite warning labels. I pull those suckers off all my cleaning products. I appreciate you all here now, and I won't ask for pity if this goes badly. I won't even ask for your approval at this point. Just wish me luck." I opened my arms wide and pouted my lips.

I accepted hugs and words of encouragement to deal with my parents and their many lectures for the evening. I listened to half, tuned out the other, and plotted my revenge.

On Monday, I took additional time getting ready for school. I wanted to look extra-hot for whatever was going down. Good or bad, I was certain to receive attention. Everyone at school had heard the story. I knew time was not on my side, so with sweaty palms, I scribbled a note to Adam during homeroom. I doused the torn-out notebook page with my then-signature citrus scent and stuffed the request in the crack of his locker.

My morning classes included a lot of whispering behind my back. I could hear my name and Adam's spoken, but I didn't see him until lunch period.

"You're right. I should. You're very right." He hovered behind me.

I straightened my spine and stared straight ahead, suspending my fork in mid-air. I felt his breath on my hair, and my icy armor melted away. I pulled out a chair to my left, silently inviting him to sit with me and the girls.

Screeching ensued as my friends scooted their chairs as far from his as they could and pretended not to be listening to our conversation.

"But, Tess, I can't leave Gina hanging. You know."

I turn again to address Rory. "I'm not completely shitty. Of course, I let him go to the prom with Gina. I settled for his counteroffer. He promised to come home from college and take me to my senior prom the following year. I believed him."

Rory nods. "Aha."

I also believed him professing he would love me forever on a sweltering July night only six weeks later.

41

After a night out with the guys, he sneaked into my yard around midnight, and I made it easy for him to pop the screen off my window and hoist himself into my bedroom. The moon reflected off my dresser's mirror, he smelled like freshly mowed grass and cheap beer, and I wanted what inevitably happened next. I truly believed giving my virginity to my graduated boyfriend would anchor him to me for eternity, and he wouldn't care about anyone else ever again.

Adam left for Stonehill in August and must have forgotten to pack my phone number. I exaggerate but hardly.

"Oh, high school, crushes, and unrequited love." Mel sighs and walks toward the kitchen.

"Immature boys," Alexa adds.

Carrie side-eyes Leah. "And confused girls."

Leah jumps to her feet. "This is a good place to stop and take an intermission!" She runs for the bathroom.

I notice a trend in her behavior, and I believe she's either avoiding us or the possibility of an interrogation. For the past few months, I've assumed she was preparing to make an announcement. Now, I'm not so sure. I don't know how long she's been hiding this from us or if she even has been. I've been too self-involved. In her absence, I dare broach the subject. "Do you think she wants us to ask her about you-know-what?"

"I'm not sure. But I don't think tonight is the right time," Mel says.

I avoid Carrie's gaze.

Carrie's sigh is the only noise in the room. She takes a long, loud sip from her lipstick-stained straw and puts down the cup with a thud. "Listen, I honestly thought she'd tell me first, but so far she just keeps dodging the subject. I don't know if she doesn't know herself, or she just doesn't want to share yet. She'll come around—or out—but only when she's ready. Let's not push tonight."

Over the years, I've sensed hints but never anything more other than speculation.

Lately, Leah's been acting more secretive. She evades questions and, when she does answer, the responses tend to be one-word quips. She admits to hanging out with other people, but she's never introduced them.

Personally, I wonder if she's met someone special. Someone she's not ready to introduce yet. I question whether we're not making her feel comfortable. I'd hate to think so, but finding out would require pushing.

I nod at Carrie's response and shake off my assumptions. I might say something I'll regret.

Leah enters and stops short of the couch area. "Y'all are so quiet. What'd I miss?"

"Nothing!" I answer too quickly.

Leah puts her hands on her hips. "Bless your heart, but I call bullshit." She smiles and heads back toward the kitchen and motions for us to follow her. "Whatever. Food's ready. Come and get it."

A stampede to the kitchen ensues.

Chapter Four

I burp extra-loudly as is my habit amongst only my girls and I feel the need for attention. This could very well be a belch-filled evening.

Mel offers a fist bump. "Class, all the way."

"Adam doesn't know what he's missing." I force another belch.

Mel squints and leans in close then backs off and points to my face. "You've got something on your chin."

I grab a napkin from the coffee table and swipe.

"No, third one down." Mel grins.

I raise my hand in a mock threat. "I'd slap you, but I wouldn't want to commit animal abuse."

Mel's eyes narrow, and she cocks an eyebrow. "Maybe if you ate some of that make-up you caked on, you'd be pretty on the inside too."

"Really? That's all you got?"

She rolls her eyes, "Oh, please!"

"You can keep rolling your eyes, Mel, but you won't find a brain back there."

"Burn!" yells Rory.

Alexa whistles sharply. "Cut the crap! What are you two, like twelve?"

"On a scale of one to ten—hell yes!" Mel puts an arm around my shoulders and points to Alexa before flipping her off.

I stick out my tongue, and for a split second, I do feel like I'm twelve years old. I feel good being silly and forgetting my sadness, even for a moment.

Alexa shakes her head. "Mature. Now let's clean up this mess. You too, children."

An empty pizza box lays open on the coffee table. The extra cheese stuck to the bottom is now a rubbery, congealed mess. Half-empty bowls of tortilla chips, salsa, and browning guacamole adorn the counter. Paper plates smeared with sauce are all that's left of the lasagna, and the remnants of Carrie's mom's fried chicken hangs heavy in the small space, replacing the previous clean smell. Everyone grabs a few items and carries them to the kitchen to toss or rinse.

I sneak off to my room. Somewhere in my closet should be a bunch of scented candles. I've received quite a few for Christmas gifts from clients over the years. Blog posts probably suggested candles as the appropriate gift for physical therapists. Hopefully one of them will come in handy now. I rummage through my closet and while reaching for a gigantic jar of pine-scented wax, I knock over a shoebox. On impact, the lid pops off, and items scatter over my pale gray area rug. I let out a loud, level-three swear word.

"Who let Tess out of our sight?"

I hear Rory yell to the others; her voice becomes louder as she nears my bedroom.

"Seriously people, major party violation."

She's been relatively quiet so far. Since she wasn't part of my shared high school memories, she didn't chime in during the stories. She opens the door slowly and asks what happened with genuine concern in her voice. I can only imagine what she thought I might be doing. "I'm okay! False alarm." I point to the objects scattered on the floor as if they were hideous creatures with sharp teeth. "Those fell out while I was getting this." I hold up the evergreen candle in my left hand and point at the floor with my right.

"Oh, Tess. You put them all away?" She bends over and picks up a small, snow-white stuffed bear. "Even Mr. Fluffy-Pants? Those gifts were given in love."

I shake my head and feel the sting of threatening tears. This box of memories has been on top of one closet or another since the night after Adam and I first kissed. I began the collection with a lone beer tab from the first night in the woods. I selected a sneaker box from the floor of my childhood closet, removing the black and hot pink running shoes I "had to have" at twelve years old. I had climbed up on my desk chair, teetering to shove the box behind an abandoned doll. With each new memento of time spent with Adam, I would climb back up and add to my treasure trove. I toted the original box to college and my first apartment. This current version is larger, having once held my first pair of tall leather boots. I keep the box just out of my reach, not to hide from others, but so I won't be tempted to delve through and get all misty or mad, depending on the day.

Rory picks up a charm bracelet and frowns. She knows the story behind every charm on the chain. All eleven.

"Can you put them back in the box, please?" Hot tears stream down my cheeks. I wondered what would trigger the waterworks, and now I wonder if they'll ever stop. I don't bother wiping them away. I know more will follow.

"No can do." She shakes her head, then turns her gaze to the mess on my floor. Her scowl softens. "Fine, but not this one." She clasps the bracelet on my wrist and squats to the floor. She scoops up necklaces and earrings, dried flowers, sappy cards, key chains, dozens of notes, and ticket stubs and dumps them back in the shoe box.

I lift my left wrist and touch the half a heart charm. The silver enamel is worn thin. Yes, at one point, we were that kind of couple. Adam used to keep the other half on a cord hung from his truck's rearview mirror. Seeing it dangling there made me feel so proud, especially when I knew he was driving around with just his guy friends. I know the memento transitioned to his night table drawer. At least, last time I checked. I wonder where it is now. If he knows. If she does.

I emit a weird sound somewhere between a choke and a cough.

Rory raises her eyebrows and points to the charm that isn't really a charm.

Adam used needle-nosed pliers to open a link and attached the tiny cubic zirconia solitaire ring to the chain. The ring isn't a real engagement ring as there wasn't a real engagement, but it served as a placeholder. I cherished it. Hell, I still do. "Yeah," I swipe at a tear. "I never did get the real one. Thankfully, neither did Brittany. Her grandmother willed hers to Brittany, insisting she wear the heirloom. Adam told me she had to honor her grandmother's wishes since her grandfather is still alive." I smirk and glance at Rory. "I'm ashamed to say I'm glad."

Rory clucks her tongue. "Don't feel bad. I'd feel

the same way. I'd even hope the setting is super old-fashioned and ugly with a tiny, dull stone."

I laugh and relax my tense shoulders and hands. I hug her and hang on extra-long.

"What are you two doing?" Mel yells from the other room. With a thump, she bursts into the room. "Don't do it! Plenty more guys are out there, Tess. You don't have to switch teams. Although Rory would be my pick too."

"You wish." Rory releases her embrace and tosses her hair.

I pull at the end of my robe hanging on the back of my bedroom door to wipe my face. I can't help but laugh at the mess I leave on the hem. Taking an audible cleansing breath, I drape my arms around both and pull in tight. I feel grounded. "How could I ever choose between you two? I'll just have to stick with guys." I don't feel ready to abandon this comfortable nest, so I lead them arm in arm to join the rest of the group.

Rory lights the hunter green candle.

Sulfur fills the air before the pine scent takes over. I forgot about the candle and am glad the distraction breaks the tension.

Carrie snorts. "Christmas? Are you kidding? It's freaking August." She fans herself with both hands.

"No offense, but you guys seriously reek." I want to present a tough exterior, but I feel it cracking. Seeing those keepsakes got to me. Especially the early ones like the ticket stubs and loose-leaf paper notes. If I was alone, I'd open the box and succumb to a full-on cryfest. I shake my hands to distract me. The distraction usually helps me, but the motion also alerts the others I'm feeling anxious.

Mel raises her eyebrows and springs into action. Grabbing Alexa by the arm, she leads her up to the table. "Hey, Al, why does Tess drink?"

"To let us know she loves us. At two am."

"Hey, Al?"

Alexa cups her ear. "Yes, Mel?"

"Did you hear, Tess stopped drinking for good?"

Alexa shoves Mel's right shoulder. "No way!"

Mel rubs her shoulder and glares at Alexa. "Yup! Now she only drinks for evil."

"Oh, Mel, I was hoping for a battle of wits, but it appears you arrived unarmed."

Mel reaches into her back pocket and produces a sheet of crumpled, loose-leaf notebook paper. "How dare you challenge me! I have plenty of ammunition." She unfolds the paper and turns to show the rest of us.

An unmistakable note I wrote and, to my sheer embarrassment, was passed around our high school in the 2007 version of "going viral."

"That's not…" Alexa gasps and clutches her chest with her right hand and throws the back of her left hand to her forehead.

I cover my burning face with my hands, peeking out slightly between my fingers. "I thought you destroyed it."

Mel grins. "I submit into evidence, The Pros and Cons of Adam Powers." She bends deeply at the waist and offers me the paper with an outstretched arm.

Upon seeing the flowery, bubbly script of my seventeen-year-old self, I gasp and feel my chest tighten. If I sniff the paper, will it still smell like the bubblegum-scented pen I was so fond of back then? I resist. I peruse the list and return the sheet. Oh, the things I could tell that girl right now. "You can do the honors."

Alexa points to Carrie who nods and disappears for a minute. She returns carrying the glitter tray now filled with multi-colored gelatin shots.

I select an orange-flavored shot because no one else will. That's how I roll. I am the accommodating friend. I feel bad for the ostracized orange.

Everyone else grabs the reds and purples.

Simultaneous slurping ensues. After years of attempts, I've determined no lady-like maneuver to consume a gelatin shot exists. Might as well just shove your tongue in there and suck.

Alexa, a preschool teacher with just enough patience, stands ramrod straight until everyone finishes licking the insides of the tiny plastic cups. "Okay, here goes. I'll read a pro, and Mel will read the corresponding con."

Mel stands, wiping her hands on her jeans. "Sorry, sticky. Go ahead."

Alexa clears her throat. "Pro: He's hot."

Her imitation of a teenager's voice is perfect. I snort.

Mel twists her hair around her pinky finger. "Con: He knows he's hot."

Alexa lifts her palms. "Pro: He's super funny."

Mel rolls her eyes. "Con: He's sort of dumb funny."

Alexa grins. "Pro: He's in college."

Mel shakes her head. "Con: He's never around."

"Wait!" Carrie interrupts. "I remember this rant being way worse back then."

"Oh, just be patient." I reach for another outcast

orange shot.

Alexa nods.

I nod back.

Alexa raises her eyebrows. "Pro: He's good in bed."

Mel winces. "Con: Sometimes he leaves right after."

Alexa turns to face the crowd. "Pro: He likes my friends."

Mel puts a hand on Alexa's shoulder. "Con: I'm not sure my friends like him."

Alexa places a hand over her heart: "Pro: He loves me."

"Con: He gets jealous." Mel lowers her voice.

Alexa wraps her arms around her middle and sways. "Pro: He makes me feel like a princess."

Mel hangs her head and drops the paper to the floor. "Con: He breaks my heart."

"Ouch, you guys." I vividly remember making the list late at night following a confusing phone call with Adam. I called his dorm room phone and heard a lot of background noise. I was alone in my bedroom and whispering so my parents wouldn't hear me. I felt worlds apart and wanted so desperately to be back in high school together. We used words like love and forever, but space and time with friends were also discussed. I don't recall who said what, but the speaker didn't matter once they were said aloud. I distinctly remember the striped spiral notebook I kept in my night table drawer for the many notes, lists, and poems I'd drafted and destroyed during high school. I drafted many versions of tonight's list, and believe it or not, I'm relieved this one remains.

"Well, we came up with a twenty-seven-year-old version of the list. Now, it's just the pros of you not marrying Adam," Leah announces from her place on the couch.

"You didn't!" I shout. Then, feeling a stab to my gut, I lower my voice. "But, what if?"

Carrie tucks her head into her neck and wags a finger. "Of course, we did. And tonight, you are way past what if."

Mel places both hands on her hips. "Would you rather I read from some other notes? You know I have them, and they are beyond embarrassing."

Leah bounces in her seat. "Ooh, like the one Tess wrote to you, and you showed all of us, about how Adam likes to be…"

"Enough!" I slice my hands through the air. "I'm sure you all remember how I liked to show off and for the record, exaggerate our escapades back in high school. Just read the new one, please."

Alexa scrunches her face. "Yes, I remember. Thanks for the visual and for the record—yuck." She lifts her phone and taps.

Rory turns her phone to face out and points at the screen. "The new list is environmentally friendly."

She takes a deep breath. "Pro: Mixed signals and second thoughts do not make a stable relationship."

"Pro: Neither of you is willing to change."

"And don't you ever," Carrie says.

"Pro: Don't stress the could haves. If it should have, it would have."

"That was mine." Rory points at herself.

She smiles and scrolls down. "Pro: You'll meet someone who is good to you. He was stupid enough to walk away, be smart enough to let him go."

Rory hands the phone to Alexa.

Alexa squints at the screen. "Pro: He's a player and never treated you like the coach you are."

"Pro: You deserve better, even if you don't believe us." Alexa hands the phone to Rory.

"Last one," Rory says. "Pro: You'll be happier."

Rory clicks off her phone and slides the device into her back pocket. She opens her arms wide.

I step into her embrace and allow myself to enjoy the support. I pull back and sigh. "Will I?" Tears pool, threatening escape. I surrender. "I'm not crying about what you guys said, your words are really beautiful, and I appreciate the effort and sentiments. I gave you license to lay it all out there, and I need to hear whatever you dish. I also need time to heal. I still can't fathom being happy with someone else."

"Only because you haven't met him yet." Leah tilts her head.

"I hope you're right, and I haven't blown my shot. Sometimes, I think I drove him away, and I'll never get another chance at love."

Rory walks closer. "You can't think so negatively, Tess. I think I can speak for all of us and say we don't, and that's why we're here."

"Totally." Leah nods. "We know you've prepared yourself for today, but that doesn't mean it will hurt any less. It's okay to admit this is sucky, but you still need to have faith you'll find someone else."

"Until then…" Carrie adds. "You have us. And as you know from experience, nothing you can do will make us leave you. Otherwise, I would have fled in 2010." She flashes a tight-lipped smile.

I sigh and sink into the couch.

Mel follows and plops on my lap.

She wipes a tear from my cheek. "You let us know what you need, and we'll take care of it. Tonight, and always. No questions asked."

I hug Mel then pull back to sniffle. So much information floods my thoughts now. I hold details that would probably shock them. If I told them, the vibe of the night could change, so at the risk of ruining whatever they have planned, I force a smile and summon my fake courage. "Deal. How about a tequila shot?"

Chapter Five

"Okay, enough Kumbaya stuff. It's my turn." Rory points both thumbs at herself while stepping onto the coffee table.

Mel hands her a brown bottle of beer with a long neck.

Rory smirks and positions the bottle under her chin. She taps the rim. "Is this thing on?"

I love her announcer-voice. I laugh and sink deep into the couch. Her humor is another reason I became fast friends with Rory. She puts me and everyone she meets at ease. Mostly, she's a listener, so when she has something to say, I know to pay attention. I'm sure her welcoming and calming presence makes her a great physician's assistant.

"Here's where I come in—college."

"College!" I say and turn to my friends.

They echo like a mantra.

One word can mean so much and conjure so many differing emotions for me. I was torn between attending college with my ride-or-die high school friends or broadening my horizons. Surprisingly, we all chose different schools. Everyone graduated, though a few of the friends took longer than four years and didn't end where they started. Now in our late twenties, we all hold degrees.

Rory glances down at her bottle. "I apologize in

advance for all the mean, awful, and accurate things I'm about to say. So pull up your big girl panties, because it's about to get real. Tess, please tell me you are in fact wearing underwear tonight."

I stick out my tongue, and she returns the gesture. Rory knows I love her and cling for fear she might leave to join her long-distance boyfriend. Her profession allows her to practice anywhere, but Rob—who she met at a health care convention—is a lobbyist who needs to live near D.C. I know it's not super far away, but I can't bear parting with my friend who has been by my side, literally rescuing me since day one at college. She's stuck with me through thick and thin.

"I was pretty pissed after I found out I was switched from rooming with my hometown friend to this girl from a public high school." Rory shimmies her body at the p-word and gets a laugh.

But I know now that was truly how this ex-snob felt when she first laid eyes on me.

"Tess arrived looking like a fake bad-ass with her vampy hair and distressed denim jacket. I immediately thought we'd never get along."

I smirk. "Little did you and your pink gingham headband know you'd be accompanying me to all the midnight teen vampire movie premiers?"

She tips her beer bottle forward.

Even now, for a supposed night on the town, she's wearing light pink capris. I know from years of living with her she can't help it. Growing up in Connecticut can affect a girl.

"Touché. But on move-in day I happened to walk in while she unpacked a framed photo of her and Adam at the beach. I thought, great, one of those girls who won't want to do anything because she has a boyfriend. I was right, but only for a short time."

"Yup." I nod several times. "Adam and I were hot and heavy in late summer, just in time to mess with my head right before I left for Fairfield."

"You didn't even go to the ice-breaker event at the dorm the first night, because you had to talk to Adam. I think I might have bad-mouthed you at the pizza party. I know I dubbed you, The Boyfriend Girl." She covers her eyes with her left hand. "People knew you by that name before they even met you."

I laugh. "No wonder no one liked me at first. I was all broody one minute and gushing about him the next." I fling my arms. "Oh my God! I just realized I really was that weak chick! Bawling my eyes out after he broke it off three weeks later made me somewhat sympathetic. You let me suffer, but the other girls on the floor listened to my sob story and told me I was too good for him despite not knowing him or even me, for that matter. Ugh, so fake. I'm sure they made fun of me as soon as they left my room. Girls suck. But at least not as bad as boys." I take a swig from my beer, slam the bottle, then take another angry slurp.

Rory gulps her beer and tilts her head. "True. Well, you can learn a lot about people when they don't get what they want. I learned Tess doesn't back down. I liked what I saw. I didn't understand your brand of crazy, but I sure admired your commitment to it." She holds up her beer bottle in salute.

I return the gesture and take another swig.

"Hear, hear!" Alexa says.

I certainly didn't leave a great first impression. Earlier that morning at home, while my parents struggled to shove the last of my stuff into their beige sedan, I clung to Adam. While they were busy, we kissed for the last time, and I cried into his chest. When the time came to let go, I hung on for dear life, both sad to leave him and afraid of what awaited me in Connecticut.

He pulled out of our hug and grinned. "I'll call ya."

No promise, no specific time, just those three words. Adam would be home for another week, free to do whatever he pleased. He couldn't move into his residence hall at Stonehill for three more days, and his classes didn't start until after Labor Day. I, however, had to report early for Freshman Orientation. So, yeah, I worried about leaving him alone, too.

During the entire ride to Fairfield, I conjured up scenarios of Adam partying and hooking up with someone else who was still in town squeezing in the last hurrah of vacation. To ease my mind, I passed the time recounting every moment of our amazing summer. Well, I skipped over a few, not-so-good memories and consoled myself by replaying his parting words.

Hours later, Rory gave up on coaxing me out to the dorm mixer and finally went on her own. For a moment, I felt bad in the silence of my room, but the thought of missing his call made me feel worse. Two bubbly girls appeared in the doorway and broke the silence.

"Hey, girl!" they said in unison.

The shorter of the two waved with both hands. "I'm Tori."

"And I'm Kelly. I guess Kelly G. cuz there's another Kelly on our floor." She giggled. "So, like, we're your next-door roomies and came to see if you want to head down to the mixer together."

Behind my back, I clenched my hands into tight fists. "Oh, hey! I'm Tess. Thanks for asking, but go ahead. I gotta do something. I'll meet up with you later though."

Tori pouted her glossy lips. "You sure? I mean, we can wait a few minutes so you don't have to go alone."

"Thanks, but my boyfriend is supposed to call. I'll catch you later."

Their spirit should have been contagious. I should have stuffed my cell phone in my pocket, followed them to the pizza party, and made new friends from the start. Instead, I foolishly thought they'd understand my dilemma.

Tori rolled her eyes and pulled Kelly by the elbow and led her toward the room on my left.

They literally moved on from me.

I closed the door and sighed. I told myself I wouldn't want to be friends with them anyway, labeling them as flakes. I passed judgment and sweated in my cramped, airless room while I unpacked and waited. I dared not turn on music for fear I wouldn't hear my phone. The silence only made me lonelier. I eventually climbed to the top bunk but remained wide awake.

Rory returned around midnight laughing.

When I heard her whisper to check, I pretended to be asleep. Despite the white noise coming from the fan attached to my headboard, I heard every ping of her phone from the bunk below me. All her new friends were IM'ing her and setting up group chats. I was still waiting for just one call.

"He never called," Rory reports to the rest of the room in a deep, mock news anchor voice.

"I know," I say to quiet the boo's, "and before one of you yells, 'Red Flag,' remember I know all about them. I have no problem seeing red flags. My problem is I'm attracted to them."

"Red flag-itis?" Carrie asks.

"No"—I shake my head—"That would be inflammation of the red flag. More like red flag-phelia or kinesis. See, I paid attention in biology." I eventually did make some great friends at college, did well in my classes, and even graduated on time. But the four-year road was not without bumps, and Adam was like a frost heave we're all familiar with here in the northeast. After he broke up with me in September, I eventually convinced myself the split was necessary. I knew I needed my space to focus at college, but a few, drunken phone calls followed, along with the inevitable hook-up over Christmas break. Still, I remained single and had some innocent fun with some other guys for a change during my freshman year.

The night I returned home for summer vacation, though, I felt like time had stood still. Hannah was beginning her first stint of dating Ryan and convinced me to go to his house on my first night home. I made accompanying her seem like a burden, but secretly I knew Adam might be there, too. Barefoot and wearing short cut-offs and a loose tank top, I descended the creaky carpet-wrapped steps leading to the basement. I hoped the noise would attract attention. I spotted Adam reacting right away.

In the musty basement, he sat on the worn-out, burnt sienna couch. He fidgeted with his baseball hat and bounced his right leg.

I didn't even try to hide my goofy grin as I reverted

to the fourteen-year-old version of me.

With a racing heart, I approached and forced myself to whisper, "Hey."

A smile overtook his face, and he mouthed a greeting.

I heard a few teasing comments from the guys. I caught sight of Adam's blush right before he dropped his gaze to his feet. Not to be deterred, I deposited myself on his lap and wrapped my arms around his neck.

"Welcome home," he breathed into my ear and gave a little nibble.

"I missed you," I whispered.

"Oh, yeah? You wanna show me how much?"

A little later in his truck, I did my best to show him, and he reciprocated. I guessed my efforts worked since I once again fell into a drama-filled relationship by the end of the night.

As fall approached, I tapped the brakes.

Adam left first to move into his off-campus apartment.

I helped him move in, and everything was fine between us, but a few days later, I called him while I was still home. "I think maybe we should not be, like, officially dating right now. You know?"

"Tess, I'm cool with whatever. You know I don't care about labels. As long as we can talk and hang out back home, I'll call us anything you want."

I'd like to say the decision was the mature move on my part, but honestly, I had thought I was merely beating him to the inevitable punch.

"You know what they say about mistakes—performed more than once they become a decision,"

Rory says.

I didn't want to start off my sophomore year behind the eight ball as I had before. I knew I was lucky Rory stuck by me. I point to her now. "Remind me to ask you one of these days why you stick around."

"Don't go getting all gushy. I just have a weakness for needy things. I think it might be an actual clinical condition. For the past ten years it's been you, and someday I'll transition to stray cats, and I fully expect you to arrange the intervention and pay for the therapy."

We laugh now, but I did count myself lucky that Rory took pity and agreed to live with me again. Fortunately, Rory scored a suite with two other girls she hit it off with, and who tolerated me. Not Tori and Kelly, because I'd burned that bridge right to the ground. Too bad, too, they turned out to be pretty cool. I was fully aware I had an uphill climb with these second-chance roomies. I arrived at our new four-man suite on Labor Day with puffy eyes.

"Why?" Carrie interrupts. "I thought you said you were the one who ended it?"

"Yup. I did, but I was still a wreck." I felt physically ill imagining whose arms I might have sent him into—with permission.

I plopped my bags in the hall and hugged Rory. I wore a skirt to show effort, and I had even bought one of those floral, monogrammed, quilted duffels to fit in with the rest of the preppy crew.

She pulled out of the hug and squinted. "How are things with Adam?"

I winked. "Who?"

Only then did Jen and Katie emerge from their

bedroom.

"Hey, girls!" I waved and then pointed to my eyes. "Word to the wise, make sure you're not allergic to adhesive before wearing false eyelashes." I laughed and reached into my duffle bag. I produced a bottle of cheap champagne with a wide smile. "Happy New School Year?"

Katie nodded and softened her apprehensive scowl. "I'll go find some glasses."

We kicked off our new living arrangement off with a bang. For the record, drinking and decorating do not go well together. Our posters and framed photographs remained askew and eighteen inches too low for the entire year as a reminder.

I was spared a Christmas break reunion with Adam courtesy of my parents surprising me with a cruise through the Caribbean islands. They told me the trip was a reward for keeping up my grades and my mind off Adam during the first semester. I wasn't dumb. I knew the cruise was a ploy to keep my hands off him during vacation too.

Sure, more drunk calls were made, and I spent many late nights awake missing him, but I held out. Sort of. An incident occurred, and I hope it goes unmentioned tonight, but I highly doubt these girls will omit this roast-worthy event. Still, I cross my fingers.

"You swore to me you were over him." Rory points. "But I should've known you were just waiting for the summer."

I shrug. "What can I say? I became an expert at hiding my plan to relapse, like any good addict." I snap back to the present and slam a hand on the solid wood coffee table. The sting reverberates through my whole body, alerting me I am quite buzzed. "God, what is it with us? Me? Me. Why did I always go back for more?"

"Don't ask me." Rory points to herself. "I never got how you could always go back and never let anyone take his place. But, then again, the rest of us wanted what you two had. I mean, when your relationship was good."

Carrie lifts her plastic cup. "True that."

"I never knew whether to envy or pity your relationship," Leah adds. "But yeah, the good times rocked."

When the relationship was good, it was great. I felt most comfortable when I was with Adam, just hanging out and sharing inside jokes. I liked when my friends included him. I took pride in being the "cool couple." Then one of us would do something stupid, or just think we were getting too close and retreat. This charade continued throughout my college years. I remember these amazing summers, like romance movie type-stuff. We lingered at the beach to watch the sunset and talked about a shared future. Oftentimes, I brought lunch to him at work, and I spent time with his family at cookouts and baseball games. Those times felt genuine.

The summer before my senior year was epic, and the good times persisted through October. Adam had graduated, and I thought we'd stay together for good.

He talked of the future and a life together even while sober, so I felt like his words were true. That fall was my turn to get scared and not return his phone calls. I found avoiding him easier to tolerate from my college cocoon. By the time I returned at Christmas break, he was hanging out with his new work friends acting all superior and adult-like.

"But you allowed him his space, and he eventually came crawling back," Alexa interjects.

"Yes, he did." I nod then keep my head down. "He always did. Except this time when it counts."

Chapter Six

Leah slowly, and a little unsteadily, saunters over and drapes her arm around my shoulders.

Sensing Leah is about to perform one of her horrible impersonations, I stiffen.

"Just when we thought you were out, he pulled you back in."

Her southern drawl kills the delivery. I respond, even though I don't want to encourage any more impressions. "True, but most of the time I let myself get pulled in." I throw my hands in the air. "Hell, I usually tossed him the rope."

Afraid Leah will continue with the performance, I reach over and smack Mel on the back of the head to get her attention. I'm confident she'll get the hint, plus she's the only one in striking distance.

Mel touches the back of her head, but then her eyes widen, and she nods. "Wait, I've got one I don't want to forget. Sorry, Leah." Mel stands briefly, falls back onto the couch, and makes a second attempt in one motion. She twists her mouth the way she does when trying to remember something. "Right, okay. Got it. With Adam, you have completely mastered the right way to do everything wrong."

I cock my head. "You sure you slurred that right, Mel? Sounded like a compliment."

Mel scrunches her face and mouths the words

silently.

Alexa leans in and pulls Mel back on the couch. She thrusts her own bottle of water into Mel's hands.

"Anyway, I made some smart decisions with Adam. Remember, I didn't move in with him. I held strong." I pound my chest now but will forever question my decision. I might come across as tough and confident, but I second guess myself as much as the next person. In this case, I still wonder if moving in with him would have kept us together. I steer my thoughts back to the present company and resume faking a tough exterior to keep the vibe of the story rolling for everyone else's benefit.

"Aren't you glad you listened to us—that one and only time?" Alexa asks.

"Sorry, girls, but Hannah gets the credit for influencing my final decision." I was twenty-four, and Adam had just turned twenty-five the first time moving in together was discussed. I had recently secured my entry-level position at Athletes in Motion, and Adam was working for his second construction company. We had degrees, jobs, money, and friends. I had the clear advantage with my living situation. I shared a great condo with Hannah in an ideal location while Adam endured a revolving door of temporary roommates in an overpriced, mediocre apartment behind an MBTA station. The dark rooms were always filthy and reeked of dirty, boy feet. I wasn't surprised at his request for me to move in. I saw right through his romantic gesture.

He broached the subject one fall night at the Phoenix, our group's usual bar.

I sat next to Adam at a sticky square table for four, and Hannah and Ryan had just left to refill our pitchers of beer. They were gone just long enough to discuss life-changing decisions. In classic Adam fashion he blurted, "We've had this rocky relationship thing going on for like ever. What if maybe we move in together; it could be like a test, ya know?"

Eloquent he's not, but I knew his request represented a monumental step in the commitment department. Despite the obvious upgrade I would offer as roommate and housekeeper, I was thrilled at the prospect of moving forward with our future. I didn't want to turn him down but knew I should. I loved sleeping over and waking up in his arms, but I also enjoyed the clean, germ-free bathroom and floral scent at my place. Needing time to choose my words, I slowly took the last warm swig of my beer.

I scooted my chair closer. The dragging caused a loud screech, and I winced, then composed myself and leaned in to kiss him. I kept my face close to his after the kiss so I could hold his gaze. I wanted him to know I was sincere.

He took a deep breath.

"I'd love to, I really would, but my parents would flip. They just started to like you again and might even believe we're meant to be together. I don't think I should push them right now." I felt disappointed he'd chosen this moment to ask but hopeful he felt so confident about us and hoped he wouldn't be too upset with my response. I sank back in my chair.

The corners of his mouth dropped, and he exhaled. "Are you refusing because you want to be engaged first?"

I hesitated. This response was not what I was expecting. The mention of a proposal made me feel giddy. I fought to conceal a smile and pursed my lips. Unsure of how best to respond, I muttered, "Not exactly."

"Because if that's what it will take…"

I jumped to my feet. "Whoa! Don't even say the words jokingly here. I promised in Vegas the next time you asked my answer would be yes. So the next time has to be the real, official one."

Adam grasped my elbow and guided me back to my chair. "Settle down, I wasn't going to propose here and now." He chuckled. "Give me some credit."

I leaned in and kissed him again. "I'm sure the real thing will be epic. I love you."

Adam placed a hand on my knee. "If you love me, then move in with me."

"Sorry. I can't." I grasped his hand in both of mine. "Really, it wouldn't go over well with my parents. We'll have to proceed in so-called traditional fashion."

The corners of his mouth dropped, and he looked away. After a minute, he turned back and nodded. "I get it. I'm glad you respect them, and I will, too, but I still think sharing a living space would be good for us."

Hannah and Ryan returned carrying fresh pitchers.

I dropped his hand and scooted my chair back to the original position.

Adam stood and took the pitcher from Ryan. He refilled our empty glasses.

I couldn't move on as easily as he seemed to be doing, and I fought to act as if we hadn't discussed anything major.

Under the table, Hannah tapped my foot and then mouthed, "Did you two have a fight?"

Smirking, I picked up my phone and texted her.

—LOL pretty much the opposite. Explain later.—

Hannah's phone buzzed from her pocket. She read the message, shook her head, and repocketed the device.

I wasn't lying about my family to justify remaining in my cushy accommodations. For a long time, my parents didn't trust Adam. As I'm an only child, my parents were very involved in my life. I can't and didn't hide much from them. During the high school years, they knew about every breakup and were usually correct to assume if I was either crying or stomping around the house Adam was to blame. Even from the safe distance of college, they always knew what was going on or not between us. A combination of the small town and the fact we'd introduced our parents long ago made keeping our status a secret nearly impossible. If we moved in together, they would know before I started packing. At the time, I didn't feel ready for such drama. Then again, sharing an apartment might have been better than continuing the walk of shame I performed several nights a week. But I held out, and a year later, I was glad I had not given in.

That said, when I got the nod from Hannah, I knew I had scored big. I had only just moved in with her over the summer. I was personally flattered she asked me to share her fabulous condo and by extension invited me into her life of privilege.

I first met Hannah at field hockey practice in ninth grade and fell instantly in awe. Now, with no siblings to have to share with, I'm not lacking for anything materially or in the attention department, but Hannah gave off a vibe of having it all. Moreover, she was so pretty—later, gorgeous—I assumed she had a perfect life. While the rest of us were in the midst of filling out, breaking out, and unsure how to act, Hannah was silken of hair and smooth of complexion and composure. And to boot, she was always sweet to everyone. She made it impossible for anyone to hate her. I yearned to be her, and since I couldn't, I wanted her to be my friend.

The first week of high school was our third week of athletic practices. The dreaded double sessions were a grueling morning run, practice, then weight training followed by a lunch break and an afternoon of scrimmages. Even though I could barely walk after the week, I made the cut for the junior varsity field hockey team. At the first after-school practice, I remember being a sweaty, stinky mess. During a water break, I pulled up the collar of my T-shirt to wipe my face and heard an unfamiliar voice calling to our coach from across the field. I squinted and saw a slim, leggy girl wearing a trendy, maxi sundress with oversized designer sunglasses pushed up on her head of auburn hair.

After a minute, she approached the field.

Our coach met her halfway.

The majority of the team, me included, stopped our chatter and stared. From the way we gawked, you would've thought we were the boys' football team.

After a brief exchange, our coach led her to the team awaiting instruction on the next drill.

I had spilled water from my squirt bottle down my athletic-gray shirt, so not only did I have visible pit stains, but a long dribble line down my chest. Attractive.

"Hey, team, this is Hannah Fallon," she said.

Hannah gave a cute little half-wave, and I

remember telling myself to try out the move as soon as possible.

"Hannah's family just moved here from Chicago and wants to see what field hockey is all about."

"My old school didn't offer this sport, but it sounds like fun," she added with a perky voice.

"Hey, we all suffered through double sessions and tryouts," our tough-as-nails goalie, Joanne, said.

Hannah's eyes widened. "Oh, I understand. That's okay, I'll try next year." She took a half step back.

If Joanne challenged me, I would've run away at top speed, but Hannah simply thanked the coach and turned on her heels.

"Wait," our coach said to Hannah's back and then turned to address the team. "Hannah's family literally moved here over the weekend, and she registered for classes today. I think she deserves a chance."

Hannah inched forward and flashed a perfect smile.

After a grumbled agreement from Joanne and a cheer from the rest of us, our coach asked who would like to show Hannah the equipment and explain the rules of the game.

I boldly stepped forward and raised my hand high, sealing my chance to guide the new girl.

Of course, Hannah was a natural, and everyone adored her. I fell all over myself teaching strategies of the game she could have easily figured out herself. The next year, she became our JV captain and held the coveted title through moving up to varsity for junior and senior years. More important to me was her title of my friend. I made sure everyone knew I was the one who discovered Hannah.

On her first day of school, everyone else's second,

I sought out Hannah at lunch and invited her to sit with our group. She never left what became our usual table.

Everybody wanted to impress Hannah. I exhibited my best behavior the first week and threatened the others to follow while she sat next to me in the cafeteria. I was hyper-aware she could dump our group for a cooler one at any time. I desperately wanted to tease her about her accent, but I bit my tongue when she pronounced her o's like a's and stifled the urge to correct her whenever she asked if anyone was "going with?" or "coming with?"

"Yeah, you taunted me instead," Leah quips.

"You made yourself an easy target…darling." Carrie mimics her drawl.

"Bless your heart."

We've learned that when said the right way, the southern statement is equivalent to F-U. Despite the addition of Hannah, our group was off to a rocky start at our new school.

"Right." Mel turns to Rory now. "See, we lost Juli and Sarah to another group."

"Yup." I nod. "They pulled away over the summer then sealed the deal on the first day of school, sitting at the swimmer's table and ignoring us. In likewise mature fashion, I ignored them and flaunted my new shiny toy. Hannah more than made up for the double loss of the others."

"You recruited me, too, don't forget." Alexa sits straighter.

"I thought we poached you," Carrie says.

"Sorta." Alexa shrugs.

She had spent half her time with our group and half with another since junior high, but I encouraged her to

73

join field hockey. Once Hannah was on board, Alexa stayed loyal to us. Thanks to Hannah, our six-pack was complete. Rory is the chaser I picked up later in college.

We discovered Hannah had older twin brothers who were freshmen in college. One brother studied engineering at MIT while the other pursued pre-law at Harvard. Hence their move to Massachusetts. Her parents were afraid she'd miss her friends back home and become a depressed teen, so they constantly welcomed us to their house. Her basement became our home base, and her parents our favorite. They had access to tickets to anything from pro football and basketball games to backstage at headlining pop-star concerts.

Aside from providing perks, and more importantly, Hannah was a good and loyal friend who loved to have a good time. She even stayed with me after discovering I didn't belong to the coolest clique. Hannah went north to the University of New Hampshire for college, and I visited her as often as possible at the sorority where she became, no surprise, the president of her chapter.

After college, Hannah joined her family business as expected. Her father and his cousins manage commercial real estate all over the country. At first, Hannah made coffee and copies and learned the ropes. She eventually obtained her real estate license. When her parents decided it was time for her to live on her own, they invested in a new building in the city near the North End and bought a few units.

"When she asked me to join her in one of the newly finished, modern condo units with a doorman and underground parking for an embarrassingly low monthly rent, I felt like the Chosen One. I was transported right back to our field hockey days. What can I say? She's fun to be around, opportunities fall in her lap, and I still wanted her to like me, even in my twenties. So naturally when Adam asked me to move in with him, I wasn't immediately interested. I liked living with Hannah and certainly didn't want anyone else taking my coveted spot."

"But Ryan eventually did," Leah says.

I sigh. "By then I felt obligated to surrender my spot. Over a year had passed and Ryan continued asking Hannah to move into his cruddy place. I would never have allowed her to live in that roach-infested flop house. Hannah was too nice to ask me to leave, and I felt duty-bound to move. Plus, Alexa's crazy internet-listing roommate needed kicking out."

She salutes me. "I can never thank you enough for saving me from Psycho."

I shake my head. "She was no Hannah."

"She wasn't human." Alexa shudders at the memory of the girl who spoke only to herself and someone named "Azriel" under her breath.

My cleaning OCD was a welcome addition to Alexa's apartment. Thinking back, that's probably when the urge transitioned from a mild condition to full-blown obsession. I moved into the room previously inhabited by Psycho and, as warned, I had my work cut out for me making the dark, smelly place tolerable. I immediately traded the choking scent of incense with the calming aroma of ammonia. I performed an exorcism with air freshener and fans, replaced the lost-cause carpet, and painted the walls a calming shade labeled "cloud."

Adam said he understood why I moved in with Alexa, but he continued asking me to live with him. The offers usually came when he was at my place at two in the morning or he was locked out of his apartment. Again, usually at two in the morning.

I continued to refuse him and kept my promise to the girls. "Hoes before bros."

"And so on and so on until this past year." Rory rolls her pointer finger in a circular motion.

My stomach tightens again. "Right, and then the fateful night, again at the Phoenix." I look at my non-existent watch. I left the real one on my dresser because it was a gift from Adam years ago. "Speaking of, let's head over there soon." While not quite dark yet, the light is fading. I hope the temperature drops with the sun, too.

Carrie gazes into her cup and swirls the straw. The ice cubes clink. "Who knows what will happen there tonight? I mean, so much has gone down in the Phoenix, for all of us."

She's had a tough time being a minority within our extended group of friends. A major minority she calls herself.

The Phoenix is a dive bar with a pre-and post-college crowd. They don't play dance music, but that doesn't stop us from shaking it. Still, for Carrie to meet other black guys, which is her admitted preference, she needs to hit the city clubs. I occasionally tolerate the thumping house music for her. Years back, she dated one guy who loved hanging with us at the Phoenix, and our group practically adopted him. Trevor was everything Carrie wanted, but staying with him meant moving to California and away from us. His job opportunities after he finished grad school here in Massachusetts all came from Silicon Valley. He begged Carrie to go with him.

I tried to support her, but when she announced she could never leave her family for California, I was relieved. I know she referred to her single mom and younger siblings, but I'd like to think she meant all of us as well. She dated a few white guys, too, but her weakness is for black guys who can dance. Her test is to go to clubs like Paradise and The Alley to see who can keep up with her.

Still, Carrie usually comes with us to the Phoenix, and she was there the night I enabled everything to change. I remember the night at the Phoenix all too vividly. I've replayed the conversation so many times in my head. I still wonder if I did the right thing and question if keeping my mouth shut would have landed me in the long, white gown today. "You know, that night was the last time I danced with him. And now..." I picture Adam walking out onto the dance floor in his tux, then force the image out of my head and recount the night my future altered.

I arrived at the Phoenix separately from Adam as we came straight from our respective jobs. Adam and I weren't together per se, but even apart, I still felt like we were something. I spent half the night drinking and talking with friends, both with him and individually. The crowd was typical, mid-twenties. The usual smells, stale beer and men's body spray as an attempt to cover up the workday. And of course, I remember the usual sounds. A local band played old high school and college favorites. Once buzzed, my body found his on the dance floor. Mind you, the dance floor is merely a ten-by-ten-foot area where tables and chairs had been cleared. I shuffled around in a normal dance fashion, then advanced to grindy as the music changed. We transitioned to kissing and moved in unison toward the line of cast-off chairs against a wall.

Adam plopped down first.

I settled in next to him. He rested his head on my shoulder. His head felt heavy, not the usual, comfortable familiarity.

We both sat still for a moment, then he lifted his head.

I turned to face him. "Adam, what are we doing?"

He shrugged. "Heading down that old familiar road?"

I let out a large puff of air. "Yeah, but should we? It seems like we're treading water. I don't know." I pulled my sweaty hair into a top knot and swiped my forehead. "I do know our back-and-forth, vague relationship is not fair to either one of us. As bizarre as this might sound, I'd find walking away easier if I knew you had someone good for you." Just remembering I said those fateful words now makes me nauseous.

Adam tilted his head and cocked an eyebrow. "Oh really?"

His disbelief made me brave or stubborn, I guess. Either way, I got riled up and stupid. "Yeah, someone like…" I scanned the bar and spotted a strawberry blonde I'd never seen before at the Phoenix, and I figured her to be a few years younger than me. She leaned against the bar with two other unfamiliar girls, all sipping their Long Island iced teas daintily through straws. They stuck out like sore thumbs with their perfect make-up and designer purses hanging mid-thigh, insignias facing out.

I took a breath and spat out, "Like her." I pointed at the girl who, of course, turned out to be Brittany.

"You can't be serious," Adam scoffed then squinted to get a better view of Brittany.

After taking a second look, I noticed her flawless figure.

Now, I wish I had just laughed and punched his arm to let him know I was joshing. Instead, I put my hands on my hips and tried my best not to slur. "Try me."

He's been doing so ever since. I sniff several times.

Leah makes a "T" with her hands. "Time out, drama queen. Your version makes for a good story, but they didn't start dating that very night."

I shake my head. "No, but it was the first time Adam saw her, and I told him to go for it, so in my book that was the night everything changed."

"But your book has footnotes. You hooked up after they got together."

I want to keep a poker face but feel the corners of my mouth creep up. "I absolutely kept my foot in the door—his door. I wasn't giving up that easily. Duh." Recalling a few late night appearances, I blush deeply, though I don't feel any regret. Maybe only regret for not pursuing him. Could I have prevented tonight? Should I have? Oh, God. Alcohol and remorse—is there a more lethal combination?

"Confession time," Carrie announces. "How often did you answer the booty call after they got together?"

I snap out of self-loathing. "I admit to a couple of indiscretions, but they were necessary tests to make sure he was making the right decision."

Carrie grunts. "And is he?"

I sigh. "Making the right decision? The decision is not mine anymore. I gave him my permission and promised I wouldn't interfere anymore. It's over." I turn to swear, and tears flood my eyes. Whether I'm swearing at myself for crying, for letting this happen, or for what I wish I could say now, I'm not sure.

After a moment, I feel a hand on my back and then another, and one on my shoulder until all five hands are on various parts of my body. I sink into their arms. After sobbing and snotting all over them, I pull back.

"I should clarify here that I did not pursue him after they became engaged. Some lines I do not cross. But there's vital information you don't know. I swore, swore I would never tell. If I told you all now you'd understand, and I really, really want you to know this fact, but I promised I wouldn't betray his trust. Believe it or not, I still value loyalty."

"Tess," Mel says, "It doesn't matter now. You can tell us anything now."

The rest of the girls nod.

I place both hands over my heart. "I know I keep repeating those words, but this promise matters. At least it does for me. I might have broken little promises, those kinds you make thinking you'll keep, like never looking at another guy. Life-altering promises like this one though, no I would never betray him."

"You are too good for him," Carrie says.

"No, that's not why she's there and I'm not."

Leah sweeps her arms around the room. "Since here is where *we* are and if you tell us, you might feel better…"

"Telling you guys would only make me feel better

tonight. I'd eventually feel guilty for telling you. Nothing can change the facts now. I could have if I'd acted on it, but I didn't." I sniff. "Believe it or not, I didn't think he'd take the engagement this far."

Rory raises both eyebrows. "Seriously?"

I press my forefingers under my eyes to catch the lingering tears. "Pathetic, I know. But honestly, if you knew what I know, you'd understand, and that's my own dilemma. I can't share. Don't bother asking."

Rory offers a box of tissues. "Okay, we won't pressure you."

I grab a handful and blow my nose. "Thanks, I just need a minute." The weight of the memory makes me feel dizzy. I settle into the couch and close my eyes to allow the fateful night to play out before me. Maybe if I relive the pain, I can let go, but I must do so silently.

Six months ago, I heard a rare knock on my apartment door. Not a normal knock, more like a hesitant tapping. "Who's there?" I wasn't expecting anyone, and friends usually texted upon arrival. I pretty much knew where my girls were that Sunday morning—asleep, church, or the gym. Our monthly Bitches' Brunch was scheduled for noon, and each of us had our own method of preparing. I'd just started a load of laundry and was arranging my hair into a ponytail in anticipation of my three-mile run.

"It's me," the familiar voice answered.

"Hang on, Adam!" I snapped the elastic into place and opened the door. "C'mon in. What's up?"

"Uh, okay." His eyes widened into saucers. "I guess you don't know yet. Is your phone broken?"

"What now?" I put my hands on my hips. "God forbid I shut down my phone to update and charge.

What earth-shattering event happened on social media I missed? One of you idiots get arrested last night?"

He shuffled his feet. "No, someone got engaged."

"No!" I screamed and ran into the kitchen. I grabbed my phone from the counter. I needed to power up from the hard shutdown. "I can't believe Hannah didn't call me. I knew Ryan was taking her somewhere special last night, but wow. I wasn't expecting this."

Adam grabbed my arm holding the phone. "Tess, don't look. Let me tell you. Please. It's not Hannah and Ryan."

My stomach immediately lurched, and I became sweaty. "What? No."

Adam nodded.

My knees wobbled. "What, Adam? What happened?" I needed to hear him say he did not ask Brittany to marry him. She was just supposed to be a distraction. She'd already been around too long.

He still held my elbow. "Let me explain." He led us both to the couch.

I pulled out of his hold. "You proposed to Brittany?" I practically spat. "Brittany?"

"No, I didn't."

"What then? You implied you're engaged."

"Yes, it appears so."

I crossed my arms over my chest. "Cut the shit and spill."

He removed his baseball cap and ran his hands through his hair. "Sorry. Yeah, um. You know from the night you and I, well…you know. I meant it when I said I was planning to end things. Okay, so I had been avoiding her calls for a couple days and knew I was being shitty, so I texted her on like Thursday suggesting we should go out by ourselves and talk or whatever."

"Uh-huh." I made the speed-it-up gesture with my left hand while my right held the now-buzzing cell phone.

"Right, so I was fully prepared to ask her to slow down and maybe suggest taking some time off, etc. Well, she insisted on meeting at the restaurant, which was weird enough, but then I get there and she's all dressed up fancy and made up, ya know? She was acting all weird and jumpy. Finally, after I picked at my food, I said, 'Listen,' and she interrupted me abruptly and said she wanted to beat me to it and blurts out, 'Will you marry me?' I was all like, 'What? What are you talking about?' Then two servers ran over and gushed and yelled, 'OMG' and asked if we just got engaged. Brittany told them yes and hugged them. I found out later she knew them in high school."

"So, like, yesterday?" I scoffed at the time. I foolishly believed he would end the story by saying he told her she was nuts and never wanted to see her again. Obviously, I was mistaken.

"Whatever, Tess. Listen, what happened next is messed up. They grabbed her phone, and Brittany smooshed in next to me, and they took a ton of pictures. Next thing I know a cake was on the table, and her phone was dinging like crazy."

I widened my eyes. "The servers posted on social media?"

"Yeah, and I assume her friends were waiting to re-post."

"Of course," I say.

"I didn't even say anything, never mind yes. I put down all the cash I had so I could run out. I don't know if I under or overpaid. I grabbed her arm and led her out to the sidewalk and asked what had happened."

"We just got engaged, silly."

"Ugh, I can actually hear her." I continued taking the news lightly and joked because I thought the situation was over. I figured he just wanted me to hear the whole story firsthand.

"Well, anyway. Brittany pushed out her bottom lip and said in her baby-voice, 'Unless of course you don't want me, and I'll have to go take everything down.' "

"I said we needed to talk, and she took it wrong and said I had nothing to worry about because she promised her grandfather she'd wear her grandmother's diamond, and she could figure out dates later. She acted ridiculously happy, but in a self-absorbed way, so she couldn't even hear my protests or see I was in shock. I suggested going to her apartment to talk, and I planned to set her straight, but when we got there the place was filled with her squealing girlfriends. I guess she either told them or they saw on social media. She ran to her room and came back wearing the ring as if the engagement was all legit."

I jumped to my feet. "What are you going to do?" I leaned over and grabbed him by both shoulders. "You can't go through with this!"

Adam hung his head. "I know. I'll set her straight."

I pushed his shoulders back in hopes he'd meet my gaze. "That sounds like you haven't done so yet. What did you do?"

Adam gently took my hands from his shoulders and stood. He still looked down. "I snuck out once they all got wasted and had put her to bed. I went home and tried to get a hold of you all night. I ignored everyone else texting and calling. I slept like two hours this morning and came here."

I wiped my sweaty neck and shook my head. "Now what?"

He finally met my gaze and fiddled with his mangled hat. "I don't know. I came here hoping you could help."

I laughed. "My ex-boyfriend who just got engaged to someone else wants my advice on how to escape? Do I understand correctly? Or did you want a recommendation on where to honeymoon?"

Adam put his hat back on his head. "Tess, seriously. I need your help."

"Fine. I'd give her the whole day, but you'd better end this charade tonight. She just wants the attention, and she'll be just as happy to get the negative attention tomorrow when she posts #jilted, or some other stupid hashtag girls use for pity phishing."

Adam took a step back. "Wow, she's not that shallow."

"Oh no?" I stepped closer and shook my finger close to his face. "Just watch. Sorry if I sound callous about a girl who just trapped you into matrimony."

"Hashtag: sorry, not sorry?"

"Ha, ha. Yes."

"Okay, I feel better." Adam reached into his pocket and removed his car keys. "Go for your run and enjoy bitchy brunch or whatever you girls do today. Please don't tell them what really happened or what I told you a couple of weeks ago about ending it with her. I'd rather leave Brittany with her dignity still intact."

"Fine!" I sauntered to the door.

He placed his hand over mine on the doorknob.

"Tess?"

His touch felt reassuring. I turned my face toward his. "Yeah?"

"You're the best." He kissed my cheek and smiled.

I'd felt so smug and confident and had set out on my run remembering a recent conversation. Just a few weeks prior, Adam confessed that he and Brittany had nothing in common, and the attraction had worn off. This inside information fueled my confidence. How naïve. I had wanted so badly to share the admission with my girls.

Later, at brunch, they must have thought I was nuts. As soon as I walked into the back room at the restaurant, I was ambushed with hugs.

"I'm so sorry, girl!"

"OMG, he must be crazy."

"I think the whole thing was spur of the moment. I heard he didn't even ask her dad's permission."

I silently groaned. Keeping the truth was killing me, and I craved correcting my friends' misinformation, but knowing it would be over the next day kept me grounded. Alexa hadn't come home the night before, and I had many questions for her, but she got to me first.

She squinted. "Are you okay?"

I nodded and feigned a pout.

Carrie grabbed the arm of a server passing by. "Get this girl a mimosa—stat!"

I shook my head. "I'm fine. Honest. A drink couldn't hurt, though."

Carrie stuck her hands on her hips. "What are you hiding, Tess? Or taking?"

"Nothing. I probably just haven't processed the

information yet."

Leah joined us and passed around various cocktails. "That's for sure."

Bloody Marys and mimosas turned into beers at the bar during football games. I staggered home at ten and texted Adam.

—Wanna come over to celebrate your new freedom?—

He replied an hour later.

—can't.—

I panicked and grabbed my phone. I pulled up Brittany's page and read, *Status: Engaged to Adam Powers*. I texted him.

—You chicken out?—

—For now. long story—

I threw my phone onto my bed. I desperately wanted to call Mel or Hannah, but I still didn't think I could confide in anyone. I promised I wouldn't tell, but he promised he'd end it, so why should I protect him? Afraid to jinx the situation, I kept quiet and prayed my silence would pay off.

Two painstaking days later, he called.

I missed the call and listened to his long-winded voicemail message while on a jog. With each lame excuse, my pace quickened. I surpassed a personal record that afternoon.

He'd gone to her apartment to set things straight and was once again hoodwinked. Her parents were there for dinner to celebrate. Adam left promising to make a good husband, and he would check his calendar for August.

I deleted the message, and I immediately texted him.

—WTF?—

My phone rang, and my heart skipped a beat. If it was over, he would've just texted. He was calling.

"No worry. I plan to explain to them how, in fact, *she* asked me. I think they'll understand. The whole misunderstanding will be over soon. What's the big deal? You know the truth. Relax."

"Relax? Ha! I can't tell anyone else, and it's killing me."

"So, it's about you?"

I clenched my hands into tight balls. "Ugh, Adam! That's not what I meant."

"Riiight."

"Adam!"

"I gotta go deal with stuff."

Click.

We didn't talk or text for the rest of the week. Brittany's status remained status quo until today. Today, wedding bells framed her profile picture. Below her name read: *Update: Marrying Adam Powers*.

Chapter Seven

Tears sting my eyes, and I blink rapidly to hold them back in, but I feel myself losing the battle. My breath quickens, and my hands begin to twitch. I need to act swiftly, or I'll segue into a full-on ugly cry session. I throw my head and arms back as if stretching, and announce casually, "I'll be right back. I'm just running to the bathroom."

Alexa pushes me back down into the couch. "No way, Train Wreck, we have not reached your station."

"Seriously, please trust me. I'll only be a minute. I won't do anything stupid."

"Moo!" Leah announces through cupped hands. "I call deja-moo."

"Okay, Leah, what is deja-moo?" Rory asks.

"When you know you've experienced this bullshit before."

"Ha, good one, but I really have to pee." Having delivered the words, I summoned the urge. "You may escort me to the bathroom or face the consequences. And you know I don't mean wetting my pants. But an accident might happen anyway." Sarcasm feels temporarily soothing.

I glare at Alexa, who is not getting up. I hope she'll get the message I'm holding a big secret, and she should think twice about messing with me.

She promised once this weekend passes, she'll

confront Hannah. Well, she and Hunter both will. Hunter is one of Hannah's older twin brothers, and not only have he and Alexa been secretly dating, they recently made a down payment on a house. Preschool teacher Alexa is anxious to have her own kids to care for, and Hunter is all too willing to give her the white picket fence and crumb-filled minivan. They progressed very quickly, but Hunter is a go-getter. Like Hannah, he's gorgeous, smart, and successful. Basically, he's the whole package. In the past, Hannah has been very opinionated about who her brothers date, so this will be interesting, and I wouldn't miss the reveal for anything.

"Hey, Al, I forget—did you say to go ahead and share? Or don't you dare?"

Alexa purses her lips and hoists herself.

Mel shuffles closer. "Hand over the phone then, Tess. No texting Hannah from the potty." She rests one hand on her hip and extends the other. Then she turns her head to face Alexa. "Sorry, I don't trust you either. She clearly has something on you."

Alexa crosses her arms over her chest.

I clutch my phone. "C'mon, you know I can't help but wonder what's happening at the wedding. You know, besides the obvious." Again, I try to sound callous and uncaring on the outside and not wounded like I feel inside.

Mel glares back. "Not your circus, not your monkey."

"We're your circus monkeys." Leah giggles and scratches her armpits.

I secretly hope the wedding is turning into a circus. I imagine fighting families, drunken groomsmen, and crying bridesmaids. I grin and deposit my phone in

Mel's palm a little harder than necessary on my way to the bathroom. "Whatever."

Over my shoulder, I announce to the entire group, "I wasn't going to text Hannah. I know she's under strict orders not to answer any texts or calls from me tonight. Believe me, I don't want to hear about the ceremony or tacky reception anyway."

I'm totally lying, and they know the truth. I will hear all about the wedding. I can't avoid being told, but not from Hannah or trolling social media posts. Darcy will be anxious to explain every minute detail. I can just picture her now beaming in her frilly, white flower girl dress. She had proudly given me another fashion show two weeks ago.

"Am I beautiful?" Darcy's pigtails bounced while she twirled in the organza and tulle creation. She giggled at the swishing sound.

"Of course, you are," I told Adam's little sister. She did look beautiful, but she's not so little anymore, and my voice caught as I realized how grown-up she looked even in the dress designed for a much-younger girl. She's almost thirteen now, and her body is starting to show it, but she'll forever act like a four-year-old due to a chromosomal abnormality. A thirteen-year-old would roll her eyes, mortified to be seen in such a babyish dress and asked to drop rose petals as she walked down the aisle. Not Darcy, she's thrilled to be part of the ceremony.

"I like Brittany," she said into the air.

I sensed she was recalling the trip to the bridal store where Brittany told her to pick out anything she wanted. I'd heard the story recounted numerous times. She usually segued once she put on the dress.

Thankfully, Darcy doesn't read facial cues too well and never picked up on the wince I made each time.

Darcy likes clear answers and affirmation, so I put aside my opinions. "And she likes you." I offer a tight smile.

"But I wish you were the bride to Adam. I forget why not."

I unclench my teeth, but my stomach hurt delivering the rehearsed answer. "Thanks, Darce. Remember I told you? Adam and I are just good friends now."

"Oh right. I know." She moved on to arranging her collection of miniature dolls.

She likes rows and arranged two perfectly straight ones. I believe the process makes her feel in charge. Years of spending afternoons with her and reading numerous articles have helped me to understand a fraction of the intercepting thoughts competing in her brain.

For once I was thankful for her short attention span.

"Let's hang up your pretty dress so it doesn't get all dirty." I unzipped the dress while she sorted dolls and simply stepped out of the poufy pile on the floor. She would've been perfectly happy to remain in her character underpants and socks for the rest of the day, but I slipped a T-shirt over her head and guided her legs into polka dot shorts as she sang a nonsense song to the ponies she held in each hand.

"How about a snack before Mommy comes home?"

"Popcorn!" Darcy dropped the ponies and dashed toward the kitchen.

I caught her climbing on a chair to reach her favorite bowl. I deposited her on the floor while I placed the popcorn bag in the microwave and braced myself for the burning butter smell which I can't stomach.

Darcy jumped anxiously counting down with the timer. "Ten, nine, eight…"

I poked a straw into her juice box and handed her the drink. She calmed while I pulled out her chair with the booster seat she no longer needed but refused to surrender. I scolded myself, remembering I should've encouraged her to insert the straw. Her parents advised me to allow her to do more things for herself, even if trying meant mistakes and spills. "Independence with supervision" had been the family motto for the summer. Darcy was starting a new school in the fall and needed to meet some milestones. Milestones for a toddler. During my thirteenth summer I stuffed my bra and chased her brother.

"I'm home!" Mrs. Powers entered the kitchen and placed two reusable bags on the counter and removed the groceries.

"Hi, Mommy! Can Tess stay?"

I froze. "Thanks, but I have to go today, Darcy." I usually stay a bit longer than necessary so she doesn't see me as just another babysitter or teacher, but the friend I truly believe I am. However, I wasn't in the mood to run the risk of bumping into Adam. He knew my regular Thursday hours at his parents' house.

Mrs. Powers remained focused on sorting the groceries and spoke quietly. "Got a minute to talk?"

"Um, sure." I instantly became worried. I have a close, yet casual, relationship with Mrs. Powers. Much easier than anyone would probably imagine I'd have with the mother of my ex-boyfriend. When I'm at their house, I'm Darcy's friend. Still, anytime an older adult asks to speak with me, it's unnerving, and I assume I've done something wrong and fear the worst. My supervisor at work knows to open with, "Everything is fine, no worry…" Of course, those words still make me want to barf.

Darcy turned to study her mother, and her eyes widened. She can sense other's stress levels and is very empathetic. "Do you want me to watch a video in the other room?"

Mrs. Powers straightened from her hunched position over the bottom freezer and smiled. "Great idea, Darce." She leaned down and kissed her daughter's head. "Do you remember which color buttons to press to make it work?" Colored duct tape constituted the most recent tool in the arsenal of aids to help Darcy with independence.

"I remember! Bye, Tessie, see you next week." She gave my middle a quick hug before darting away.

Mrs. Powers' smile faded, and she pinched the space between her eyes. "Next week is actually what I want to talk to you about."

"Okay." I caught my breath and searched for something to do with my hands. I scooped up the popcorn kernels surrounding Darcy's bowl.

"My family, you know my sister from Seattle and her kids? They're coming here to stay next Thursday."

"Ah." I nodded.

"I'm sure you'd still be a big help, and Darcy will be expecting you at the usual time, but I just can't ask that of you. It will be…"

I held up my hand like a stop sign. I wanted to spare her feelings. I also didn't want to hear her apologize. "I get it—wedding central. How about you just text me if Darcy is being stubborn? I can pick her up and take her to the mall or a park or something to distract her."

Her face softened, the stress clench of earlier erased. "Your plan sounds good. Thanks for understanding." She opened her arms.

I accepted the hug. Her embrace seemed longer than our usual greetings or good-byes. I felt genuine compassion.

"Thank you for everything, Tess."

"No problem." I averted her gaze and casually walked out to my car. I drove a block away, pulled over to the curb, and parked. I dropped my head to the steering wheel and sobbed uncontrollably.

When Adam and I first started officially dating and talking on the phone every night, he told me about his little sister. He explained she was a lot younger. His mother had been at high risk when she became pregnant after a long battle with secondary infertility. By the time we started dating for the second stint, Darcy was just shy of two years old, and his parents were worried because she wasn't babbling or making any eye contact. She walked independently, but she bumped into furniture and fell a lot. A year later I still had not met her, but I knew of the dilemma her parents faced. Start testing or wait and see? When they suspected seizures in her sleep, they made an appointment at the children's hospital in Boston to perform an overnight EEG.

Even though he genuinely worried, Adam still threw a party at their house that night. It was epic. I think the idea was primarily Ryan's and Tyler's. Nothing like peer pressure. While his parents awaited Darcy's fate, his friends played quarters at their kitchen table all night.

I did go home eventually but returned in the morning to help clean the mess. Epic party meant epic mess. I immediately cleaned the kitchen and sprayed air freshener throughout the house. At noon I was vacuuming the hallway and barely heard Adam alert me when he saw his parents' car pull into the driveway. I dropped the vacuum. "Oh my God!" I had yet to meet his parents and didn't know what, if anything, Adam had told them about me. This was not how I pictured our introduction.

From the other room, he called. "Get in here and make it look like we're watching a football game or something."

I peeked my head into the room and saw Adam hurdle the leather sectional.

"I can't leave out the vacuum. That's a dead giveaway."

He picked up the remote. "True. Hurry."

When I heard the TV come to life, I wheeled the vacuum back down the hall and into the closet where I'd found it earlier. When I asked him the location, Adam had no clue. I had to hunt. I heard the knob turn on the door connecting their attached garage to the house, and I panicked. Heart thumping, I ran into the bathroom and, a minute later, realized my mistake. I couldn't hear anything and therefore didn't know when it was safe to emerge. I didn't know if his parents were still in the room talking to him, but I didn't want to look like I required the bathroom forever. I flushed and ran the faucet before I took a deep breath and carefully walked out to the family room. I desperately hoped Adam would give me a script to follow.

"There she is!" Mrs. Powers extended both arms as she walked toward me. "Adam was just telling me he's helping you study for a math test."

I was relieved his mother came to my rescue, but I was unsure if she wanted to shake my hand or hug me, and the uncertainty caused me to stop short. I felt awkward but was instantly relieved by her welcome and annoyed with Adam's lie. Sure, Adam was a grade ahead, but any tutoring would be coming from me. He should still be sending me thank-you notes for writing most of his papers throughout high school and college. Funny how I would get a booty call the night before an important assignment was due or if he hadn't read a book he knew I had.

"Yes, hi, I'm Tess." I composed myself and recalled my father's advice to always look a new acquaintance directly in the eye upon introduction. Hers are the same warm brown as Adam's and equally inviting. I was so thankful for the ease of the introduction; I released my hands from their clenched state to offer a handshake. I hoped they weren't sweaty and fought the urge to wipe them on my pants.

"Well, it's nice to finally meet you." She shook my hand, tugged her sweater, and touched her hair. "Sorry I'm a little, well a lot, frazzled."

Adam cleared his throat. "Where are Dad and Darce?"

"She fell asleep in the car, so did I for a minute, but he wanted to let her wake on her own." She finished explaining.

I heard a door slam. An older version of Adam appeared carrying a lavender-blanketed bundle. He was taller and less rugged than his son, but I could see the resemblance.

Mr. Powers made the 'shh' sign.

He must have gotten sick of waiting in the car.

Adam's dad gently laid Darcy on the couch next to Adam.

Mrs. Powers motioned for the three of us to walk a few feet away from where I met Mr. Powers officially.

After our introduction, he excused himself explaining he was dying for a shower.

Mrs. Powers asked if Adam and I would keep an eye on Darcy while she made lunch and asked what kind of sandwich we'd like.

Once she was out of earshot, I finally got to address Adam. "Oh my God, they are so cool about me being here. I thought they'd freak."

Adam squinted and cocked his head. "Why?"

I fiddled with my ponytail. "I don't know." I didn't want to admit I assumed he'd been keeping me a secret. I followed him to the sectional couch. I settled next to him in the coveted wedge portion.

Adam picked up my hand, intertwined our fingers, and held our hands on his thigh. "Tess, they know all about you."

A smile spread across my face, and I blushed to the roots of my hair. I remember being blissfully happy, which probably explains why I was so approachable when Darcy woke up only a few minutes later.

Soft, slurpy noises made me look her way. Her large, honey-brown eyes popped open and scanned the room. Once acclimated she crawled over from her section of the couch to where we sat and climbed onto Adam's lap.

He kissed the top of her head.

She sank into his chest.

Her baby-fine hair was a mess, staticky on one side and matted against her head on the other. I guessed from her car seat. The tiny hospital bracelet cut into her chubby wrist.

She plopped her thumb into her mouth and with her free hand pointed at me.

I couldn't help staring and grinning like a fool at her drowsy expression.

"Darcy, this is Tess," Adam said.

She looked directly at me and narrowed her tiny eyes.

I smiled.

Darcy looked back to Adam.

He nodded and tapped her nose.

She turned to me, removed her thumb from her mouth, and held it to my face.

Adam laughed. "That means she likes you. She's offering you her thumb."

"What do I do?" I whispered.

"Nothing. She'll put it back in a second."

Instead, I touched my thumb to hers and popped mine into my mouth.

She smiled wide around her own thumb and re-deposited the soggy digit.

By the time Mrs. Powers joined us in the family room with a tray of sandwiches, chips, and sodas, Darcy was in my lap. I can't explain the immediate attraction. I have no siblings, only a few older cousins, and at that time, limited experience with babies and toddlers. She felt comforting in my arms, and I felt confident holding her. My earlier anxiety slipped away while I inhaled her powdery, baby-scent.

Mr. Powers entered the room wearing fresh clothes and toweling his damp hair. "Wow, she likes you!"

"She's so sweet," I said.

"Do you babysit, Tess?"

"Dad!" Adam scolded.

I shot him a dirty look and turned my attention to his father. "I do, and I'd love to watch Darcy anytime."

And so began our Thursdays together.

Needless to say, I fell hard for both of them on the spot. Witnessing his compassion for Darcy made me feel even more attracted. Adam and I haven't had a smooth, uninterrupted relationship, but Darcy and I have.

My time with her made me realize I was interested in, and I thought I had a skill for, helping others. During my senior year of high school, whenever someone asked about my future career plans, I gave the standard, "I don't know yet," response.

Mrs. Powers was the only one with a suggestion. She asked if I'd thought about working with kids with special needs. I wasn't so sure about teaching per se, so I entered Fairfield as "undeclared" in the fall. The school was my father's alma mater, and I grew up as a fan of the institution. Applying there made sense as it felt familiar, and the campus was not far from my family, but still allowed me to move out of state. Hesitant to leap to declaring a major, I took the freshman prerequisites and two early education classes. I didn't hate them, but classroom teaching didn't click. Ultimately, a knee injury sealed my fate. While playing tennis right before sophomore year final exams for part stress reliever, part procrastination, I ran for an overhead shot and turned my upper body before my right knee got the message. I heard a loud pop and dropped to the ground. I hobbled to my finals on crutches and had my meniscus repaired the day after I moved home for the summer. Three weeks later, I entered a physical therapy center and was immediately intrigued by the machines and methods of strengthening, stretching, and healing. The next semester I selected health studies and reached out to my PT instructor who I later interned for and followed when he opened his own center.

Darcy had taught me I could truly help others with their difficult challenges, but she will always be the only special girl in my life.

Chapter Eight

"Open up, Tess. I can hear you crying. We're here for tears too, you know. Not just debauchery."

I ignore Rory's pleading from the other side of the door for a few minutes and give up. No use staying in the bathroom conjuring up memories if I can't share them, so I open the door and let Rory pull me into a hug. We shuffle awkwardly together into the living room.

"Oh, Tess. Don't cry. Remember—this too shall pass." Leah's drawl is so thick the statement sounds like a sampler embroidered on a pillow in her grandmother's South Carolina parlor.

"Yeah, it might pass like a kidney stone, but it will pass." Carrie laughs and picks up her phone, taps a button, and repeats the phrase. Yup, she records what she considers clever quotes. I wonder if she's planning a career in stand-up or plotting a tell-all memoir. Both are possibilities with her, and each scare me equally.

"Geez, Care, the joke wasn't that funny." Mel waves her hands in the air. "If you want a good one, try this—Life is not a fairy tale. If you lose your shoe at midnight, you're a sloppy drunk."

"Heard that one before," Alexa says.

"How about an Adam roast?" Rory asks. "We should stop calling him your Ex. We should call him your Y. Like why did you date him?"

Their attempts at cheering me up are futile at this point, and I let the tears fall before wiping under my lashes where I imagine mascara has run. If any remains.

"Damn," Rory says. "I really thought my roast would help."

"Sorry, I was thinking about Darcy." I lie.

"Here." Alexa hands me a tissue from the box on the table. "Never mind them. You and Darce will always have a special relationship. Don't go doubting that one."

She loves kids and has been teaching three-year-olds since graduating from Lesley. For her, the call to teach emerged early. She insisted on playing school in her bedroom despite having just come home from real school. Afternoons at her house, I wanted to watch cartoons in her cool basement or play on her swing set. Our playdates continued to include an imaginary classroom at her kitchen table because I could be bribed with stickers and freeze pops.

"Thanks, girls." I blow my nose loudly and punch Alexa's arm lightly. "Somebody better get me another drink or start a story before I bring all you bitches with me into the depths of depression."

"On it. We love you too, Tess." Rory hands me a beer and holds hers up in the air and raises her voice. "You are only as strong as the drinks you mix, the tables you dance on, and the friends you party with."

"Then I must be a warrior. Just watch out for me if I get out of control." I point to myself with both thumbs. "I wasn't equipped with brakes."

"Base model." Leah snorts.

Mel stands and puts her arm around my shoulder and squeezes hard. "I hope you're serious about being strong because it's confession time. We decided that what happened in Vegas has stayed in Vegas long enough. Tonight, you tell us what actually happened on the last night of the trip."

I knew I'd have to come clean one of these days, but I didn't expect to confess tonight. The eager look on my friends' faces, wide eyes, and anticipatory smiles should scare me, but little do they know it's not a scandalous story I'm protecting, but a heartbreaker.

"I still think they went to a chapel," Carrie announces.

"I maintain we did not get secretly married." I pause and wink at Carrie. "But I never said we didn't go to a chapel."

Leah slaps her thigh. "I knew it!"

A few years ago, Hannah and Ryan had arranged a group trip to Las Vegas. She invited all us girls and a couple of her coworkers who I knew from happy hour get-togethers. Ryan invited all his guy friends, which of course included Adam. I might have omitted that detail when I told my parents the plans. They were nervous enough about our group of girls, so I figured I would spare them the boyfriend factor.

To this day, I don't know if they are aware he was on the trip. I thought the admission would be one of those funny stories Adam and I would tell them one day once we were married with kids. I pause now, realizing the exchange will never happen.

With the combined groups, we formed a large, obnoxious collective.

The flight attendants had their hands full with our section of the plane. They ran out of their cheapest light beer before the plane crossed the Mississippi River.

Adam and I were officially together at the time, and I looked forward to our first trip which didn't also include our parents or Darcy. I planned for weeks. I spent all my free time working out and shopping for new summer outfits. I knew Adam was excited too because Darcy repeatedly told me she was happy Adam and I were going to Paris. Adam had shown her online photos of Las Vegas, and the image etched in her brain was the replica Eiffel Tower at Paris Paris on the strip. I sent her a postcard of the casino and bought a miniature paperweight version.

Although I was excited to travel with my boyfriend, I promised the girls I would not be glued to Adam. He likewise made it clear he would need ample guy time, so I figured he made a similar oath to his friends. I suggested the best way to prove our loyalty to our friends would be by not sharing a hotel room.

He sighed. "I know you're right but wish you weren't. I'll tell the guys to make room for me."

"Sorry to be the downer, but a room for just us would be insanely expensive, too." I smiled to hide my disappointment.

Adam and I did manage to sneak some time alone during the day. While everyone was drinking at the pool, I snuck off to meet him but returned to my assigned room each night. Except for the last night, the night in question—hence the interrogation.

"The last I saw of you was at dinner," Alexa recalls. "Then you magically reappeared at the airport in the morning." She makes a poof sound and throws up her hands in the air.

"When you showed up in the terminal, every one of us looked at your left hand," Rory admits.

"I noticed." I shoot my middle finger in the air, then smile, and replace it with my ring finger. "But don't forget, you went missing the night before along with some guy from Hannah's office."

Rory blushes. "How could I forget? I wonder whatever happened to Matt." A smile spreads across her face then she snaps back. "Damn, you almost distracted me. You are evil. This is not my shit-show. Now, tell us where you disappeared."

I let out an audible sigh, knowing I have no choice but to confess. Still, I know how to stall and mime drinking from an invisible cup.

"I'll get you a drink once you assume the position." Mel points to the table. "Pick your poison. I'll get it."

With a glance out the kitchen window, I can see it's now dark. Time to start pacing my consumption, or I'll soon face a real intervention with counselors and medical staff. "I'd better stick with beer and water from here on, thanks." I step up on the table. "Let's see." I tap my temple slowly like I'm trying to remember, as if I could ever forget. "After dinner, we went to a pawn shop, a bar, then a psychic, a female imposter review, oh—and a chapel."

"You're such a liar!"

"Shut the front door!"

"Not in that order, mind you." I flash a wide smile.

Leah shakes her head. "I knew it, y'all. I. Knew. It."

Pillows, napkins, even an empty plastic cup are thrown.

I hold up my hands in surrender and to dodge the projectiles. "Stop! We didn't get married. Geez. We're not Ross and Rachel."

Silence, finally.

On our last night, the whole group had gone to dinner together. Thanks to forward-thinking by Hannah and Mel who made an early reservation, we had a great meal at a moderately priced restaurant. Everyone agreed it was a perfect pick, which is rare. Then the inevitable disagreements ensued. No one could decide on a plan for the evening. Leah, Carrie, and the work-friends wanted to dance all night at a club. At least that's what they told the group, but I knew they meant to hang out at the bar of a cheesy club and allow guys to buy them drinks, lose them on the dance floor, then hook up with a hot guy they knew they'd never see again. Or was Leah looking for a girl? I'm confused now.

"Gambling, baby, that's why we're here." Ryan high-fived the guys seated to either side of him.

Hannah shoved Ryan's shoulder. "Oh, please. Just because you won a few bucks you think you're all experts now."

"When we hit a jackpot, remind me not to share."

Rory, Mel, and Alexa had tickets to a show at nine, and they hoped the rest of us would meet them at a hotel bar for late night.

Adam, seated across the long table from me, kept quiet.

I followed his lead. Everyone was talking over each other, and no one noticed our silence on the matter. I exchanged eyebrow communication with Adam until I excused myself to the bathroom. I hoped he would get the hint and follow me. I waited in the hallway between the kitchen and restrooms.

He rounded the corner two minutes later. He

grabbed me around the waist and pulled me in close. "I left enough cash on the table to cover us. Ready to get out of here? I'll text the guys later. They'll never notice I'm missing if I ghost now."

I kissed him quickly and put my arm through his. "You read my mind. Or my eyebrows. I'll send cryptic emojis to Mel in a few minutes. Let's go."

"Where to?"

I squeezed his side. "Let's not start again."

"No worry, this is Vegas—bad ideas are everywhere. I'm sure one will find us."

"Blackjack?" I asked.

"I gave up. I suck at it. You know, math."

My arm still hooked through his, I pulled in closer to avoid oncoming foot traffic and to take in Adam's familiar, comforting scent. It's my favorite fragrance. I even rank it above bleach.

"Let's just walk down the strip for now. I'm so full from dinner I need to move. Like you said, a bad idea is bound to jump out, and the odds are higher on the strip."

"Yeah, probably the highest anywhere. No, maybe New Orleans."

"We'll add Mardi Gras to the bucket list."

It's still on there.

The air was warm, and the sounds of excited tourists and flashes of blinking lights surrounded us. I was giddy, so light on my feet I was practically skipping down the sidewalk. He left the group to be with me and spoke of a shared future. What more could I ask for? I only had one drink with dinner because the drink prices, unlike the meal, were insane. I guess that's how they get you. The lack of booze and the nice meal left me feeling calm and content, not drunk and stupid yet.

Adam appeared happy to me too. His grin was wide, and I thought I could hear him humming. His step was unusually springy.

Then he stopped short. He apologized to the frustrated and surprised people walking behind us, and he turned. "I love you," he shouted to be heard above the sounds of the crowd dodging us.

I can still feel my smile. My cheeks stretched so far, my eyes watered. When I lie in bed at night remembering the good times, this moment always appears.

"Tess, I mean really love you. No matter how much crap we give each other, I'll always love you."

To avoid crying under the neon blinking signs, I replied, "I'll remember this conversation next time you say you can't stand me."

He grinned and sighed. "Don't get me wrong, there are plenty of times I can't stand you, but I still love you."

I pulled him off the sidewalk and into a doorway. If I was professing my love, I wanted him to hear clearly. "Adam, I've loved you since I was thirteen. I think I've made that obvious. By now, there's not much left you can do to change my mind." I squeezed his hand and met his gaze. My eyes felt wet, and I blinked rapidly. His grin took a devious upturn. A look I know well, and usually welcome.

"Tess, you'll marry me, right?" He ran his hands through his slightly sweaty hair. "I mean, ya know when the time is right and all."

I reached up on tiptoe and kissed him fiercely,

pulling him toward me with both hands.

He pulled back. "Oh, hell! Should we just get it over with and tie the knot right now?" He pulled me back in, nibbled my ear, and whispered, "I've heard rumors of a place or two around here to seal the deal."

My knees weakened, and my heart raced, but the sigh I delivered wasn't out of surrender. Of course, I'd been envisioning my wedding to Adam for over ten years, and when this trip came up, I did consider a quickie, cheesy wedding. How could I not? I didn't tell anyone I'd packed a white sundress. Fear of being teased by my friends prevented me from hanging it in the shared hotel closet, so I left it folded in my suitcase.

"Adam, I would, in a heartbeat, marry you tonight. It would be wild and fun and so very us, but I've always pictured the whole traditional engagement thing. You know?" I looked up at his face illuminated by the neon signs.

"So it's about the diamond, huh?"

I shook my head. "That makes me sound petty. I didn't mean I need a ring exactly."

He kissed the top of my head. "No, not petty. You sound like a real, live girl. I know you want to do it the old school way. Guess I'll have to ask your dad and all that."

"Yup, not just the old school way, the hard way." I tried to sound upbeat.

"I get it," he said and looked away.

I reached my right hand to his left cheek to turn his face back to mine. "No for now, but the next time you ask, my answer will be yes." I stretched to tiptoes once again and kissed him softly. "I promise."

"Deal." He took my hand.

Back out on the sidewalk, he swung my arm playfully for a few minutes until foot traffic came to a halt and stranded us. A line for a concert at one of the big casinos blocked our way. I didn't recognize the name of the band on the sign, but months later I would see the group again on the Grammys. Whenever I hear one of their songs, I think of that night and wish I'd said yes.

Taking my hand and the lead, Adam guided us around the crowd and down a small side street. Filling the space were two pawnshops, a souvenir store, a liquor/convenience mart, and a storefront with a neon sign advertising Palm and Tarot Card Readings.

Adam and I turned to each other without saying a word. Using the eyebrow-raising and head nodding method we'd perfected earlier, we agreed to enter the storefront at the end of the alley. The space could easily have housed a drycleaner in the past.

I gripped Adam's hand a little tighter and entered a small, dark room. I heard a chime as the door closed behind us. The air appeared smoky, but I only faintly smelled incense. The room was furnished like a Victorian parlor with clawfoot, velvet-upholstered chairs. A heavy, dark purple curtain with gold rope tassels hung in a doorway across the room from where we stood frozen. Faint music played, more like light chiming. A single lamp on a card table barely lit the room.

I've seen enough cartoons to expect a turban-wearing gypsy to emerge from the curtained doorway. Images of my favorite cartoon rabbit with purple eye shadow and gold hoop earrings carrying a crystal ball gave me a little giggle. I quieted and straightened to attention as someone very un-cartoonish parted the drapes.

A tall, black woman with extremely long, bright orange nails and matching lipstick approached us. Her Afro was held back with a silk scarf, not a turban, giving her a chic, 1970s vibe. She wore an emerald green evening gown featuring a rhinestone drop pendant in the cleavage. I fought to look elsewhere.

She clapped her hands together. "Oh, a couple. I love couples. I sensed a reason to make an exception. See, I was just walking out to flip the sign to Closed when I heard the door chime. I didn't plan to come out, but something urged me to peek. I do have to report backstage in twenty minutes, but I can't resist a cute couple. I'm as gorgeous as ever anyway. How does thirty-five bucks for ten minutes sound?"

Only then did I realize she was a he, or more specifically, he was dressed as a she. Female impersonator? Trans? Drag Queen? I didn't know the correct title for such an entertainer, especially in Las Vegas. I couldn't speak.

I mulled over terms and weighed political correctness and squeezed Adam's hand.

"Perfect." He reached for his wallet.

She smiled and accepted the money. Their hands touched during the exchange. "Thank you, dear. Ooh, aren't you the buff one? Construction. Homes, maybe roofs. Twenty-three?"

"Twenty-five, but yes to all the rest."

She beamed at us both. "I'm Zelda, for now. When I take the stage, I'll be Vivienne. Bobby when I call my mama."

Aha.

I relaxed my shoulders. Her welcoming nature put me at ease. She led us to a card table, and I accepted a chair. Once seated, I finally found my voice. "I'm Tess, and this is Adam."

"Pleased to meet you both. Now, like I said I gotta make this a quickie. I usually tell you what's jumping out from your auras then you choose palms, cards, or the crystal ball. At the end, you get to ask one important question, but you have to make it one for the both of you since time is tight."

"Sounds good to me." I looked to Adam who just nodded.

"Super, because your auras are just screaming." Zelda made jazz-hands. "I can tell you two are definitely in love. You met a long time ago, and it's been rocky, but fun and always loving." Zelda leaned forward and squinted. "You're at a crossroads. I can feel you both want the same thing, a future together, but you worry about making the leap." She relaxed her face and sat back in her chair. "Okay, now what do you want?" She pointed to the deck of Tarot cards stacked next to a scratched crystal ball and held out her left palm.

"It's Vegas, so cards seem appropriate." Adam pointed to the deck then placed a hand on my thigh under the table.

"I like your thinking, Honey. Tess, you agree?"

I turned to Adam and smiled. "Sure, why not?" I shrugged. The methods were all the same to me, and anyway I liked what she was saying so far. I still wasn't completely sold, but I was intrigued.

Zelda cut the cards and shuffled quickly while she explained she'd have to do the honors because of time constraints and would only lay out thirteen cards, not the whole deck. She hummed to herself and finally asked us to turn over one card each.

I flipped the first card. The image appeared to be a queen in royal garb of deep maroon and navy.

"The Empress." Zelda held a tight smile and tapped the card with a long, acrylic fingernail. "She could symbolize a few things, but we're combining cards in this version. Adam, your turn. Choose one."

Adam's card revealed what could only be The Emperor. His jaw dropped.

I grasped his hand, still resting on my thigh.

Zelda beamed and clapped her hands rapidly. "You couldn't have asked for better. You belong together."

I felt my face burn and my heart rate soar.

Adam and I hugged. A beeping from the back room startled me, and I pulled away.

Zelda pushed back her chair and turned her head toward the beeping. "Oh my, I gotta run. It's been fun, come back anytime, or better yet, come see me at the revue." She waggled her fingers.

"Wait!" I rose to my feet. "The one big question."

She smacked her forehead. "Yes, sorry. Go ahead."

I turned to Adam.

He silently mouthed, All you.

I turned back to Zelda. "When should we, ya know? I mean should we do it now? Wait? Where? When?"

Zelda closed her eyes for a moment, then suddenly opened them wide. "Go now, to the Cherished Chapel. But wait an hour."

"What? Go now or wait an hour?"

"Go, then wait an hour. You'll see." And then she

was gone.

Adam and I were suddenly alone. My mind swirled with uncertainty. "Do we go?"

"To the chapel?"

I felt like I just stepped off an amusement park ride. "I'm not sure. I'm mean, that's big. But maybe we should do what she says. I don't know. Anyway, let's at least get out of here."

Back in the alley, neither of us said a word.

I was too busy listening to the voices in my head. I thought we were walking toward the strip.

But Adam stopped at the corner in front of a pawn shop. "I've never been in one before, but I do love the show about the family who runs a famous one somewhere around here. Let's go in for a second and process what just happened."

It sounded like a good idea. Probably as good as anyone can find on the strip. Upon opening the door, I was hit with a gust of refreshing air from the cooling system. The shop's fluorescent lights were harsh, and security was tight. Tourists filled the jammed space cramped with thousands of items to inspect.

Adam drifted toward a display of signed guitars.

I wandered to the glass cases containing estate jewelry.

He found me there a few minutes later. He slipped an arm around my waist. "Diamonds again."

I tapped the top of the display case. "I was just thinking about all these engagement and wedding rings. Each piece must have quite a story to explain how it ended up here."

"Another reason you'd never want to start with someone else's good-bye." He took my hand and brought it to his lips. "Ours will be the real thing. I don't mean just the diamond."

My eyes brimmed, and I believed I'd never loved him more, and in the most unlikely of places. "Oh, Adam. You keep talking like that and you'll have to shell out the big bucks for the honeymoon suite tonight."

"Not a bad idea. I was just about to suggest you two get a room," a voice delivered.

We turned to find a security officer standing next to us. I didn't realize Adam and I were being so obvious.

"I'll have to ask you to back away from the display case before either of you take it any further." He smirked a bit.

I looked down.

"Sorry," Adam mumbled.

We disentangled ourselves and inched away from the jewelry case and slunk through the crowd.

Back outside under the bright lights, Adam let out a laugh. "Let's go get a drink."

"Yeah, I could use one."

I spotted a bar with outside seating for optimal people watching.

Adam ordered a shot and a beer for himself and the drink special of the night for me—a martini just sweet enough to mask the potency. Three drinks later, Adam asked the waitress for directions to the Cherished Chapel for a "visit."

She laughed and said something about being predictable. She jotted the address on a cocktail napkin and wished us luck.

After a short, but expensive drive, our cabbie

parked at a small, white, clapboard structure.

He turned to face the backseat and chuckled. "Well, you're here. Good luck!"

Adam hesitated outside the chapel, then squeezed my hand and slowly opened the heavy front door.

A couple stood at the altar, but the organist faced sideways and caught our eye. She discreetly pointed to a pew in the back.

I nodded and slid beside Adam on the aisle. I discreetly surveyed my surroundings. Only a handful of other people filled the front pews. The ceremony underway appeared to be halfway through. The bride and groom appeared very young. I guessed they were no more than nineteen. When asked to hold hands and recite their vows, I saw them exchange smiles, but something seemed off to me.

A lull occurred between ceremonies while the "preacher" and organist spoke to each other in hushed tones.

I turned to Adam. "What do we do now?" I whispered.

He lifted both hands. "We either go ask them about getting hitched or wait for the hour to pass. Or did enough time already pass while we were at the bar? I don't know. I mean, are we doing this? Maybe we'll receive some divine intervention."

"So, just watch drunk people get married and wait for a sign?"

"Um, I think that's what Zelda meant." He cocked his head.

I covered my face with my hands. "This could not get any weirder."

"Wait." Leah scratches her temple. "By then, we

must have been texting and calling you."

I gun-point. "I'm sure you were. But I was in church, so I turned off my phone."

"Please don't disgrace my Lord and Savior by calling a Vegas wedding chapel a church." Carrie makes a sign of the cross.

I mouth a meek *sorry*. She's serious, and I respect her conviction. I wave my hands in the air as if to erase my blunder. "So, back to the chapel, I'd snuggled next to Adam and watched another couple tie the knot in under fifteen minutes. They were older, much older, and I wondered what their story was—remarried or renewing? They spoke softly, and the organ played loudly, so I couldn't hear their exchange from our pew in the back. After the older couple finished, the organist—a thin woman with extremely long straight hair and a powder blue suit—approached us.

"Hi." I flashed a wide smile. "We're enjoying your playing." Her smile revealed many wrinkles, the kind, grandmotherly type.

"How sweet of you to say. I'll assume you're just watching and weighing your options?" She smiled again and patted my hand. "Don't worry, you're not the first." She lowered herself into the pew ahead of us and turned back to face us. "Lots of people come here to get married for different reasons. Most on a spur-of-the-moment decision they can easily get out of in a couple of months. Others choose this route as part of a grand plan to get it over with so their families can't get involved. There's another type. You'll meet one of them soon."

"Here?" I asked.

"Yes, you'll know. My guess is you two are afraid

if you don't get married now, you might regret not striking while the iron is hot, so to speak. I won't tell you what to do, just how you seem to me." She stood and patted both our shoulders. "Now, you'll have to excuse me, I have to help the next bride choose her music."

Bewildered, I spaced out through the next union.

The couple cried together at the end and hugged their three equally weepy witnesses. They were all dressed for a traditional wedding, and the flowers were coordinated as if planned. The music was classic gospel, and everyone sang along.

I had a feeling the bride must have known all her life the songs she would pick. I thought of the list I compiled years ago. The songs I wanted played at my wedding and reception were jotted in a college notebook. I wondered if I would still agree with my selections. I hoped the notebook was still in my memory box.

Adam caressed my hair. "The hour is almost up. What do you want to do?"

His touch and voice brought me back to the moment. Before I had a chance to answer, I heard a feeble voice.

"Excuse me, young man?"

Adam spun then stood to greet an elderly man wearing a classic black tuxedo with wide lapels.

He motioned for Adam to join him.

I watched as he put his arm around Adam's shoulders and guided him outside. I reached down for my purse—a designer fake I bought on the strip the day before. I expected to follow them, but suddenly a beautiful older woman sat beside me. The man's bride.

They were the older couple we'd seen get married earlier.

The woman wore a long, ivory, lace gown. Her hair, make-up, and nails were wedding-day perfect. I was instantly in awe and so eager to hear her story I forgot my own dilemma.

"Hello, dear. My name is Lillian. My husband, Harold, is speaking to your young man. I hope you'll speak with me for a minute or two."

"Of course! I'm Tess, and your ceremony was beautiful."

"Aren't you sweet?" She took my hand in hers and patted it. "That wasn't our wedding though. We were married here over fifty years ago. Harold and I thought it was a crazy wild thing to do. I foolishly assumed all our friends would think we were so cool and congratulate us when we returned home to Utah and told them the story. No, I was naïve. My mother took years to forgive me for not including her in the biggest moment of my life. My father was disappointed. Harold's parents assumed I was expecting. Everything was a mess. The worst part was we were truly in love and wanted everyone to be happy for us."

I removed my hand from hers and covered my heart. "Oh no, did you eventually repair the relationship with your family?"

She smiled and tilted her head. "Well, giving them grandkids helped. But not until our tenth anniversary, when we threw ourselves a party and renewed our vows in a Catholic church with all our family did we get truly absolved."

"So, you didn't get married or remarried just now?"

She shook her head. "No, the ceremony was for show. No vows were exchanged. We just chit-chatted with Mary and Chuck up there for twelve minutes or so. We'll do it again a few more times tonight."

I was still confused. "So, you do this all the time?"

She laughed and shook her head. "Wouldn't that be crazy? No, we travel here once a year, and for one night we talk to people like you and your young man. Tomorrow night we'll play roulette. Tonight, though, I'm willing to bet quite a few people will be disappointed if you and your fella return home hitched. How are my odds?" She elbowed me.

The image of Darcy's adorable face popped into the forefront of my brain. My parents, Adam's parents, and all our friends would no doubt be pissed. Not a stellar start to a marriage, I imagined.

I squeezed Lillian's hand. "Thank you, Lillian. You gave me clarity."

"My pleasure dear," she said.

I heard the chapel's heavy door creak open.

Lillian waved to Harold. They walked toward each other, meeting in the aisle. Lillian laced her arm through his, and they proceeded toward Mary and Chuck once more.

Adam stood in the back, rubbing his eyebrows.

I walked toward him. He looked so cute in his confusion, I had to refrain from making a joke. I halted a foot in front of him. "Well?"

Adam shook his head. "I have no words."

"All I know is our future does not begin here." I pointed back toward the altar.

"Amen." He kissed me and had led me outside to one of the many cabs idling outside.

I pause and smile now at the memory of the promises we made to each other snuggled close in the cab. I'll keep those to myself. Especially the part about planning to name our future kids Lillian and Harold.

"So, they were like the wedding-whisperers," Alexa says.

Her voice pulls me back to the present. I deflate. "Something like that. I think of them often."

Rory snaps her fingers. "We should Google them."

"Y'all, I think they were ghosts," Leah says.

Carrie throws a balled-up napkin at Leah. "You watch too much science fiction."

Rory raises her hand. "What happened after? There must be more. You didn't show up until the next morning."

I laugh at how easily my friends forgive me and crave the rest of the story. "Well, of course, we just had to go watch Zelda, I mean Vivienne, after all she did for us," I say as if they should know. "I saw your texts, but no way would I ever ditch her/him at that point. And the show was a blast."

The music had been incredible. The performances and costumes were totally over-the-top. Feathers and boas, sequins, sparkles, and glitter filled the dark nightclub. I insisted on staying through all three encores, drinking ridiculous old fashion high balls, and I don't even know what else.

Zelda came over to our table at the end and introduced some friends. She told stories until four in the morning when the staff finally swept up, signaling us to leave.

I hugged Zelda good-bye and asked which way to the closest breakfast buffet.

We stopped at the hotel to pack our stuff, and I attempted to improve my appearance and odor from the all-nighter. From the cab, I texted everyone that I was fine, not in jail or a gutter as you assumed, Mel, and advised you guys I'd meet up in the terminal. "I remembered I needed a few more souvenirs for Darcy, so I dragged Adam to a kiosk before hunting for you. I grabbed pens, magnets, and you name it. That's when Adam bought me the diamond ring keychain with *Hitched in Vegas* etched on the back." I raise my wrist and caress the charm between my thumb and forefinger now. "None of you have ever looked closely enough to see the writing. Also, I pulled off the keychain part to attach it to my charm bracelet."

Rory pouts her lip. "Aw."

"It all makes sense now," Leah says.

Carrie cocks her head to the side. "It does?"

I throw my hands in the air. "Well, that's what happened. And hey, the trip was fun and successful—none of us came home pregnant or itchy."

Chapter Nine

"True, I'm surprised none of us have scars." Leah scoops several empty bottles into her arms. She carries the load into the kitchen and disappears.

I should be grateful, but I cringe. I fear she does not know to rinse the bottles before throwing them in my recycle bin. My refrigerator is too big for the tiny space and prevents me from seeing if she is simply dumping the empties in the trash. Yes, I'll probably search through the bag tomorrow.

"No visible ones, at least," Mel adds.

"Visible what?" Carrie heaves herself off the deep couch and follows Leah toward the kitchen. "Scars? Right, at least Tess never got a tattoo of Adam's name," she says over her shoulder and snorts.

The girls laugh, but I don't join in. I can't. I tilt my head toward the ceiling to avoid eye contact, but I can tell they sense my silence. Of course, they are, I am terrible at hiding my discomfort. They don't even need a roast this time. I've already turned on the grill and skewered myself. I feel the trickle of boob sweat. Rory fake coughs extra loudly, alerting the rest of my friends to what only she knows.

Mel and Alexa whip around their heads and stare with open mouths.

Mel jumps to her feet. "Tess, no."

"O-M-G, you didn't!" Carrie runs back into the

room. She picks up the closest thing to throw—a loose couch cushion.

I catch the cushion mid-air and hold it as a shield. "No comment," I reply from behind my armor in hope of lightening the mood. I know I won't be allowed to get away with not commenting and begin to dread recounting this story. I'm not proud of the permanent result, but it felt like the right thing to do at the time. Bad decisions always do. Suddenly wanting water, and more time to think, I rise from the couch and am ambushed.

Leah lunges. She tugs down the already low waist of my jeans.

My secret is revealed.

"*Adam Forever*! Are you kidding?" Alexa asks. "And on your right butt cheek, why?"

"I don't know. Righty is my favorite cheek?" My face burns, but I smile weakly and shimmy my pants back over my hips. The silence and disapproving stares from my friends stings. "Plus, *Adam Always* seemed too literary."

Rory rolls her eyes. "You mean alliteration."

The pillow I previously caught now sails toward Rory's head.

"But I'm your roommate for God's sake! How could I not have known?" Alexa asks.

"Because you're not a perv," Rory answers.

I turn and stare.

"What?" Rory raises her eyebrows. "Oh, right! I suppose now I'm automatically one?"

I feel the need to rescue her. This was my mistake. "I can't say I've been hiding it exactly, but I certainly haven't been flaunting my butt-art. Sorry, Alexa, but one friend already knowing was one friend too many. I've been extra-careful around you. Rory only knows because I took her bathing suit shopping, and she didn't fall for the jumbo bandage."

Rory raises a hand. "To be fair, I assumed it was a bite mark and immediately accused her of some very questionable acts. She thought biting was worse than the truth and ended up telling me about the tattoo to prove she wasn't gross. Or as gross as I imagined. Of course, I then had to see for myself."

"Huh. I shouldn't say I'm shocked," Mel says.

"I suppose instead of wedding dress debt I'll be paying off the cost of laser removal for the next few years." I want to keep the talk light, hoping they'll move on and not force me to recount the events leading up to this decision. Hey, a girl can dream.

"You will, right?" Rory points. "Have it removed?"

I shrug. "It's kind of pretty." I chose a flowery script.

"Tess." Rory pouts. "We talked about this. I thought you agreed with me. Hmph! Promise right now you'll look into removal."

"Or at least cover it up with something more imaginative," Carrie says.

Alexa wrinkles her nose. "Like what? A dragon?"

I wave my right hand dismissively. "Oh, please. Dragons are so last year." I still hope we'll drop this subject.

"Seriously, Tess. You know you can't keep it." Mel leans forward and turns her head. "No wonder you haven't met anyone else yet. You have to get the bad karma off your ass—literally."

"It's not so bad." I wonder why I am suddenly so

defensive. If one of the girls did this, I would be all up in their face too.

"Remember, he broke your heart. Multiple times," Leah whispers.

"Oh, I remember all right, but when I got the tattoo, he was still showing up with a glue gun." I place a hand over my heart. "Anyway, now is not the time to discuss painful elective medical procedures. This is supposed to be a party. What time is it? I want to freshen up before heading out." I push myself off my chair.

Carrie grabs me by the arm. "You're not getting off that easy. You're right, this is a party. But it's also a roast. Jump up on the table and spill the ink story, girl."

"Fine. But first I need water. Please."

"Deal." Carrie opens the fridge and lingers a moment.

I imagine the rush of cold air must feel refreshing. My mouth is dry, and I feel a slight pounding in my temples. Dehydration or guilt, I wonder. Defeated, I kick off my wedges again and resume my stance on the table. I breathe in through my nose and out my mouth audibly to signal I need a minute to find the calm required to tell the story.

Carrie hands me a bottle of electrolyte water reserved for workouts.

Thank God one was left, but what will I resort to in the morning? "Let me start by saying this happened when things were really good."

Leah makes air quotes and rolls her eyes. "The solid years."

Carrie rubs her temples. "Wait. You couldn't have had it done a long time ago or one of us would've noticed at the beach. Right?"

I feign a sad face. "You underestimate my expertise at deception, Carrie. I'm hurt."

"Sorry, I should have been more attentive to your ass. My bad."

I nod. "I'd like to say I went to the tattoo parlor on a whim, but the process was actually very planned out. Well, maybe the whole idea started as a whim. Let me back up…"

I'd met Adam at the Phoenix on a Thursday night. The crowd was underage, and I was feeling superior and smug. I had to work in the morning and planned an early exit, but at eleven o'clock, one more beer sounded like a good idea.

"I was enjoying the PDA phase, and I was still holding out despite Adam's push for me to move in with him. I liked hearing him continue to tell me how much he wanted us to live together. I was kind of torturing him, but I liked believing it kept us…"

"Shmoopy," Mel offers.

"For lack of a better word—or a real one—yes." I take a large gulp of the lemon-flavored water and wipe the dribble from my chin before I continue confessing.

"So okay, where was I? Right, I was taking advantage of the touchy, feely, and silly phase of the night. My barstool was practically touching his, and I entwined my foot around his leg. Adam had just handed Laurie a fifty to cash out. She dropped the bill on the floor while she was inspecting it for authenticity. She leaned over to pick up the bill, providing a clear view of her tramp stamp."

"Ew," Adam said.

"I know, right? She'll regret that ink in a few

years."

"Totally. No one admits it, but I think everyone regrets tattoos eventually. Except for military, those are different. They seem required. But I know I sure would regret it."

"Are you sure?" I ran my hand over his forearm. "Even my name?"

"Especially!" He leaned over to kiss my ear.

A touch which drives me wild. Drove? "I'd do it. I'd tattoo your name on me." I was shocked to hear myself say the words out loud, but you know—love and alcohol.

"Oh yeah?" he challenged. "Where?"

The way he had asked sounded like a dare.

I turn to the girls now. "You know I take dares very seriously."

"Oh, we're aware all right," Carrie says.

Rory whistles sharply. "No more sidetracking, continue."

"Fine. I don't know," I had answered. "I never really thought about it before this very minute."

"Well, stop thinking about it right this very minute. Yuck." He pulled his leg away and stood.

I grabbed his hand. "C'mon, you'd be so turned on if I tattooed your name somewhere only you could see it."

Adam ran his hands through his hair. "Hmm. What about when we break up and some other dude sees it? Would you have it crossed out?" He accepted his change from Laurie and gave her a wink as he handed her back a twenty.

I shook my head as if I'd already made up my mind. "Never."

He glanced at his phone. "It's late, and we're impaired, so no ink for you tonight anyway. Let's go home. Your turn to pick which apartment."

Adam was right, I wasn't smashed but not in a place to make lifelong decisions that night. Or maybe, ever.

Leah stands and shakes an empty bottle. "So, when did you do it?"

I sigh. "We sort of broke up a few weeks later following a petty disagreement, but after hooking up about a month later, I went straight to the tattoo parlor to *prove* my devotion. Real mature." I force another sip of the necessary water, but the liquid has difficulty passing the lump in my throat.

"Okay." Carrie purses her lips. "Q and A time. Me first. Did the needle hurt?"

"It didn't tickle." It hurt like hell.

Mel raises a hand. "Next question. Does he have one of your name?"

I shake my head and feel my lips form a tight line.

Rory cringes but still raises her hand. "Brittany's name?"

I laugh. "Not last time I checked."

"And when was that?"

"Nice try, Sherlock, but not relevant to this story. In fact, this story is over. Let's get out of here." I finish the water and easily crush the empty, eco-friendly bottle. It does not make the satisfying crinkle of the cheap ones.

"Wait!" Leah says. "Back up. You're not done. What did Adam think when you told or showed him?"

I choke on my response. "Oh, he was fine with it…" I notice Mel sitting back with her arms crossed over her chest. I stop talking.

She's staring with knitted eyebrows and pursed lips. Mel has always had a way of knowing when I am lying or, in this case, holding back details.

"I believe he told you, 'yuck' when you told him you were thinking about it." Mel raises an eyebrow. "Did his reaction suddenly turn to, 'yum' during the big reveal?"

I shake my head slowly. "Not exactly." I took my sweet time to tell, or rather show, him the artwork. I was excited at first but in no shape to display the swollen, ointment-covered mess right away or anytime in the first week. Or the second. Wow, I had no idea the area would look so gross. The third week I chickened out. Yes, I took a whole month to admit I had gone through with it. Per usual, I planned way too big a deal over revealing the tattoo. I deliberately hid my ass so I could wait for the perfect moment which never arrived. Once I felt ready, I invited him to my place for a real dinner. I prepared a recipe from a magazine I swiped from our PT office and bought a special, black lacy thong.

"Special?" Leah asks. "How could that one possibly stand out from all your other thongs?"

I turn my head in her direction and smirk. "It wasn't dainty lingerie from our favorite place at the mall. I ventured to the naughty store on Route 1."

Leah imitates retching. "Ah, gotcha. Go on, and um, ew."

"Thank you." I curtsey. "Okay, long story shorter. Dinner was meh, but dessert was supposed to be a striptease featuring my ass as the grand finale followed by mind-blowing sex and declarations of undying love." I wave my arms dramatically and roll my eyes.

"What happened instead?" Mel asks.

"During dinner, we both received texts from Ryan alerting us Tyler's band got called last-minute to fill in at the Phoenix. They wanted us there for support. I agreed we had to go, but of course I was angry on the inside and drank too much as a result. Later, back at my place afterward, I only had the energy for a quickie and passed out. No big reveal. However, the next morning he walked into the bathroom just as I stepped out of the shower.

"Oh my God, Tess, please tell me that's not real." He pointed with both hands. His eyes and mouth became matching capital letter O's.

I snapped a towel from the rack and wrapped my lower half tightly. "Right, I just happened to coincidentally get your name from the toy machine at my dentist's office. Of course, it's real." I wanted to sound confident, but my fidgeting hands and sarcastic response betrayed me. I readjusted the towel to cover all my fun parts since I sensed the conversation had turned serious.

His face softened and reddened.

The dripping of my hair on the tile floor was the only sound for a full minute.

"Wow." He stared at my wet feet and shuffled his own.

"Is that all you have to say?" I was tempted to drop my towel to entice him to look up but was grateful he was looking down. I was also glad I'd had a recent pedicure.

"I honestly don't know what to say." He finally looked me in the eyes and cocked his head to the side, half-shrugging. "Um, thank you?"

"Ugh, I hate this part because then I asked 'Are you mad?' I wanted to punch myself for sounding so weak, but you know how quickly doubt steps in and just takes over. At least I do. I'm an expert at making the bitch feel welcome."

"Not mad, just surprised is all. Uh, I'm gonna be late." He pointed to the sink I was blocking with my towel-clad body. "Can I brush my teeth?"

Angry he carried on like any other normal morning, I re-wrapped my towel tightly and left Adam to his dental hygiene. He didn't require much grooming for a day on the construction site. I knew his routine. He'd buy a gigantic cup of caffeine and sugar from the convenience store on the corner, then drive his pickup to the day's location. Despite his college degree, he was still performing grunt work. His endless class hours spent year-round to graduate on time hindered his ability to obtain on-the-job experience, so he was catching up post-college. Though frustrated, he knew he was doing the right thing. Adam was the only guy from his group of friends to earn his degree in four years, and he prided himself on this fact. When rejected at interviews for project managerial positions, he simply refocused. Thus, he poured concrete and hauled lumber for a construction company in hopes of redemption. Eighteen months later, he'd wear a shirt and tie, but that morning he'd still donned grungy jeans and a black T-shirt.

I shrug and step off the table.

"Wait. End of story?" Mel points. "I don't think so."

"Yup, I mean, he gave the tattoo attention later and

referred to it as my 'commitment.' One time during an argument, I told him to kiss my commitment good-bye. So, on the upside, I gained all those jokes."

Sure, I was super disappointed with his reaction, but he had warned me. I took a risk, and I'm paying the consequences now. I don't want to discuss the regret though, so I hop down to signal I'm done talking. "Alrighty then, the end. I'm rehydrated now and need a beer."

"Hold it." Rory throws her arms wide like a human blockade. "Not so fast. Are you planning to have it removed?"

"Honestly, I'm not there yet. Hey, maybe I'll have your name added to my other cheek if you move to D.C." I wriggle my eyebrows. "JK, I know I should remove it, and I know I was impulsive and stupid, but for some reason, removal seems like an even bigger decision than getting it in the first place. I'll get there. I assume."

"Well, that's why we're here. After tonight, you'll be ready. We'll help. I'm sure we have some more roasts for arsenal."

"I hope so since I believe I just roasted myself with the tattoo story." I lick my index finger and touch my ass while making a hissing noise. I hope this gesture will put an end to the discussion with a laugh.

Silence follows.

I let out a sigh.

Mel clears her throat. "Does your…"

I point with a stiff arm. I raise my voice. "Don't say the dad word. You will not bring my dad into this. He would be mortified. I would be mortified. Do I have Daddy issues? No. Just a wonderful relationship I cherish but sometimes test. He can never know about this." I feel my eyes watering and the need to make a joke. "Unless of course, I require money for removal." Despite my previous tirade, I cock my head and smile.

Visions of my dad finding out have kept me awake many a night. I imagine the disapproval in his voice as he says something like, "Well, you're an adult making your own decisions now." Which of course makes me feel like I'm twelve and incapable of making even a simple decision like what candy to eat first on Halloween night. Whenever I'm doubtful, I become sad for not having a sibling to confide in, but I console myself believing I could just as easily have a vindictive sister who would use my vulnerability to her advantage. I'm grateful to have supportive girlfriends and such a great relationship with my dad, but sometimes the closeness poses its own set of problems—like having a secret.

"Okay, then. One last look?" Mel asks.

I turn around and slowly ease down the right side of my jeans.

"Bow chick-a-wow-wa," Leah sings.

I yank them down completely and lean over, mooning them properly. "Who are the pervs now, ladies?"

Chapter Ten

Carrie stands. "Ahem," she says several times.

I turn and face her directly. "Yes, dear?"

"Tess, everyone has the right to be stupid sometimes, but, girl, you are abusing the privilege." She takes a noisy sip from her plastic cup.

The rest of us wait.

I'm sensing she has more to say and feel my temperature rise.

"I've decided it's my turn. I have a roast, too, but no one asked me. Typical." She smiles with her whole face and tilts her head.

Leah groans and rolls her eyes.

Alexa knocks back the rest of her beer.

Rory motions to the coffee table. "Sorry, Care. The floor, er, table, is all yours."

Carrie nods and steps up on the table. "I'm pretty certain Tess thinks no one knows about this, shall I say, indiscretion." She puts both hands on her hips. "And I can understand why. It's a good one."

My pulse races, and I gulp. I don't keep a lot from these girls. How could I? I have kept an event to myself though. I'm hiding something I'd hoped to never reveal. But now, I make the connection between this embarrassing event and Carrie seamlessly. I just hope Carrie is thinking of something other than what I imagine. I'd welcome anything else. I try to escape the deep couch.

With a stiff-arm, Alexa pushes me back down.

I sink into my seat, but I can't keep still. I cross my legs, and my right foot bounces rapidly.

Carrie points. A harsh point accentuated by her fake, talon-like fingernails. "You're not getting out of this one, naughty girl. I know you know what I'm about to share. You're lucky I kept this information to myself all this time." She winks then turns her attention to the rest of the girls. "Now, let me start by saying if you ever find yourself in a situation with Tess as your voice of reason, just say your prayers and call your mother."

"Okay, good one, but c'mon now. You are a terrible tease. Roast her," Leah orders with a wave of her hand and a slight slur.

With her all-teeth smile, Carrie appears to be loving the spotlight and tosses her head back. I swear she'd carry a microphone if anyone let her. No stage is safe with her around.

"Well, I guess this was during one of the college summers, so maybe that's how she got away with keeping quiet. Rory was probably back home in Connecticut with her preppy friends, and I think Leah and Hannah were on one of their do-gooder trips building huts in Appalachia or something. Anyway, I was home working for my aunt—you know the beautician? I was wash-and-sweep girl for tips…"

"For the love of God, get on with it, Care." Mel throws a balled-up napkin. She misses by a yard.

"Nice try," Alexa says.

"Hold on, I'm getting there. So, Aunt Lorraine is married to my Uncle George." Carrie pauses and looks around the room.

Cringing, I reach to pick up the napkin and pray one last time to be spared the story I am envisioning. I hear a gasp.

Leah's eyes light up. She jumps to her feet. "Chief of police, Uncle George?"

Carrie smiles and nods swiftly. "Yes, Queen. The one and only."

Damn. Damn. My stomach clenches. "Oh Lord, I know where this is heading. Better bring me another drink." I touch my cheeks to check if they are truly on fire.

Carrie continues laughing from her perch.

Alexa returns from the kitchen with her arms full of beer and water bottles.

I'll have to explain myself after Carrie shares her knowledge of that night. I have no idea how much she's heard of the incident. I hope she's under-informed. I have good reason for repressing this one. I grab a beer and water and drain half the contents of each bottle.

"Uncle George had the pleasure of catching our Tess and Adam in a, hmm, how did he put it?" She taps her temple several times slowly. "Oh yeah, a compromising position." She turns and flashes a grin.

Carrie steps down and swaggers to the couch.

Leah takes a loud swig of her drink. "Get the popcorn. This should be good."

I take my time making my way over to replace her. I hang my head extra-low the whole time. "The official charge was indecent exposure in a public place. I think he spared us." I look up to gauge their reactions.

"Oh my God! Were you both wasted?" Mel asks.

I throw back my head and place my free hand on my hip and jut it out dramatically. I point my beer bottle with the other hand. "Please! Not to brag, but I don't need alcohol to make bad decisions."

Adam and I hadn't been dating that summer per se, but we'd been running into each other occasionally. Especially on Thursdays. That Thursday, I was scheduled to stay late at his parents' house to watch Darcy because the Powers were having a rare date night upon the insistence of Mrs. Powers' parents. Adam's grandparents arranged the surprise and even checked with me before making the reservation at an upscale restaurant in Boston. I was happy to assist and adjusted my day around their plan by getting up early to hit the gym. Unfortunately, it was the same day Grandma Lois' car had called it quits.

"She's a goner." My dad slammed the hood shut. He joined me in the driveway after hearing my futile attempts to start the engine. He patted the roof. "She served us well. I'll go make the arrangements."

"I'll miss her."

"Okay. I guess I'll have to take the day off to deal with this. I'll call for a tow right away since you're blocking your mom's car and mine." He shook his head. "You need to learn to park straight."

I couldn't help it. The car they gave me equaled the size of a medium yacht. "I'll add it to my list of *needs improvement.* Well, forget the gym, but I need to get to the Powers' house later. Any chance you can take me?"

"Sure, or Mom can." He turned to leave then pivoted back. "Oh, wait. This is the late night, right?"

I nodded.

My dad clasped his hands behind his back and squinted up at the sun. "Okay, I know how much they need a night out. Mom has plans with her friends to see some new billionaire, bad boy movie, so she can drop you off on the way, and then you can just call me later to pick you up."

I hugged him. "Thanks, Dad."

He retreated to the house, whistling softly.

I assumed he had to make calls about the car. I questioned who would have to break the news to Grandma and hoped the task wouldn't land on me. She'd accuse me of killing her car. I'd never hear the end of it.

I opened the heavy, steel door for the last time to retrieve my belongings. I spent half an hour throwing out receipts, collecting change, and shoving random stuff into my gym bag. I took a trip down memory lane without leaving the driveway. I kept one wintergreen air-freshener for posterity.

Now, years later, I touch a small keychain from an amusement park hanging from my charm bracelet. I thought I lost the charm elsewhere, and my heart swelled upon discovering it under the passenger seat amongst the crumbs that morning. I shake my wrist, and the charms jingle softly.

Since I couldn't make the gym, I took a long jog and enjoyed the summer day. Back then, I was only interning, and my hours at the PT office were minimal. I wasn't usually scheduled for Thursdays so I had plenty of time to think and ponder what to do for wheels from then on. I had turned up my nose at serving before the summer started, but now with the possibility of needing to buy a car, I wondered if Joey's Pizza was still hiring.

Later, while my dad was out dealing with the car situation, my mom drove me to the Powers' on the way to meet her friends. Darcy and I had our usual afternoon activities, then I deemed it a girls' night with a princess movie, homemade pizzas, and spa services. I couldn't stop wondering if Adam knew I was there. He was renting a filthy apartment on Beacon Street, and I knew from Darcy he came home regularly to do laundry and raid the fridge. I secretly hoped he would show up, but the idea didn't prevent me from letting Darcy give me a makeover with her glamour doll makeup kit.

Mel wrinkles her forehead. "Hold up. The one with the life-sized doll head?"

I roll my eyes. "Of course."

Carrie, with her advanced knowledge of the situation, snickers behind her hand.

Darcy's version was far superior to the one I had back in the day. Glitter eye shadow and a smartphone app were among the upgrades. She always begged to experiment on me, and I usually came up with an excuse, but since I was spending most of the night with her and only going home later, I obliged. She put a lot of time and effort into the makeover, but let's just say she won't be heading for a career in cosmetology anytime soon.

Hours later, she was tucked in bed, and I sat on their couch fighting to stay awake by flipping through the late-night talk shows. I heard the garage door rattle and straightened from my slouched position. For a moment, I let myself fantasize about Adam walking in and smoothed my hair. I heard his parents' voices, and my smile drooped, but I forced myself to perk up. This was supposed to be their night, not mine. I didn't want them coming home to a brooding babysitter. "Did you have a nice time?" I asked over-enthusiastically to mask my drowsiness and disappointment.

"We did! Thank you so much, Tess." Mrs. Powers giggled.

I wondered if she was a little tipsy. I'd never seen her truly relax.

"Oh, honey, your face looks like Darcy had a nice time with her makeup." She pointed at me while she continued to laugh behind her other hand.

She seemed drunk, and I was happy she was able to let loose for a change, even if at my expense. I touched my eyelids, and my finger came back smeared with a mix of pink and purple. I laughed and picked up my cell phone. "I'll call my dad to pick me up."

"No, it's late, so don't bother him. I'll take you," Mr. Powers offered. "I'm the DD." He hooked his thumb at his wife who was still giggling and struggling to remove her sandals.

Just as I was about to thank him, I heard another voice filled the room.

"Wait, I'm blocking you in." Adam closed the door connecting the garage to the family room. "I can take Tess home."

Mrs. Powers ambushed her son with a bear hug. "Adam!" Then she stepped back and scrunched her face. "Did you run out of food or clean clothes?" She peered behind him.

"A bed, actually."

"Huh?" his dad asked.

"My apartment is full of dorks. My roommates have friends visiting from their hometown in New York. They're playing some weird fantasy game and calling each other medieval names, so I came here to crash before the nerdiness rubbed off."

I thought everyone could sense my excitement and immediately felt my neck burn. I fanned myself discreetly.

"Well, lucky us," Mrs. Powers said.

Thought I detected a sarcastic tone in her voice, I could tell from her sappy grin she was happy to have her son home. "Me, too," I said too quickly then remembered to clarify. "For the ride, that is, um, you know." I then turned to Adam. "My car died today. For real this time."

Adam removed his battered hat and held it over his heart. "It was only a matter of time, but I'm still sorry to hear." He winced. "I hope Lois goes easy on you."

"Thanks. I haven't talked to her yet."

He nodded and replaced his cap. "Well, ready to head out?"

"Sure." I grabbed my bag from the floor, slid on my flip-flops, and followed Adam out to the garage.

He stopped short of a rubber ball.

I ran into his back. "Oof."

He turned to face me. "Oops, sorry. Wait, what's on your eyes?" Adam squinted in the dim light cast only by the overhead garage door opener. He moved closer and burst out laughing. "Oh my God, you look like a stripper."

Sure. I know an opportunity when one presents itself and couldn't resist. My flirt signal was triggered. "Oh yeah, does this work for you?" I asked in my low, teasing voice. I batted my glittery eyelashes.

His laughter halted.

I heard a gulp. A sly smile spread across his face.

He shoved his hands deep into the front pockets of his jeans.

I knew from a past, late-night, buzzed confession he attempted to hide his arousal.

Without hesitation, I unbuttoned the top two buttons of my sleeveless blouse.

Adam made a guttural noise and darted his gaze around the open garage. "Keep going," he urged, barely whispering.

I undid another button and narrowed the distance between us. Eventually, I pushed him against his father's car.

"We need to get out of here, now." He took my hand and led me out to his truck in the driveway. He opened my door and disappeared toward his side.

Using both hands, I hoisted myself into the passenger seat and quickly pulled off my top before he reached the driver's seat.

"Shit!" He attempted to start the engine while keeping his gaze on me.

I smiled my best sexy smile. I was down to only my lace bra, denim skirt, and panties. If we were playing strip poker, I would have been losing. I hate losing. I waited until we left his street before scooting closer. "Your turn."

At a stop sign, Adam whipped off his blue T-shirt and turned up the radio to a classic rock station. An old hair band played a familiar ballad. "Where to?" he asked.

I lowered the window all the way and threw back my head. "Anywhere." Uh-oh. I need to edit myself here. I take a swig and speak faster. "In the parking lot behind, no, I mean some random parking lot…"

"Hey, no cheating," Rory yells.

"It was a church," Carrie interjects. "The one on

144

Central."

Groans from the couch follow.

"We thought the empty lot would be the safest place." I shrug. "It was late on a Thursday night."

"Continue," says Carrie.

"For the record, I'm horrified." Alexa raises her eyebrows.

"Here, here," one, then all of them chant.

I take another swig of my beer. "Whatever. Do you want to hear the rest or not?"

"No, thank you. I think I got the picture." Alexa shudders.

Leah gags. "Too vividly."

"Fine, you get it. I'm done." I step down. "Oops. Gotta pee again."

"No way. Finish," Mel slurs. "There must be a reason we've never heard this one before tonight."

"Uh, yeah—embarrassment." I cover my eyes. "I'll spare you the details. Let's just say when Uncle George paid us a visit, Adam and I were both in the driver's seat."

Mel performs a perfect spit take.

Leah hands Mel a napkin. "Nice."

"Her mug shot is full-on pink and purple eye-shadow and glitter," Carrie says.

"Yeesh." Rory cringes. "Did you have to call your parents?"

"No, thank God. We were both of age and only paid a fine. Uncle George went easy on us. Around two in the morning, Adam drove me home in silence.

"My dad was asleep in his chair. I found out later he waited up for my call. He planned to surprise me by picking me up in my new, little sports car. Weeks passed before either man in my life spoke to or gave me a ride again."

Chapter Eleven

"Well, now that I've brought the party to a screeching halt, I'll exit stage left to the bathroom so you can discuss what a pathetic mess I am."

Mel holds up her hand and shakes her head. "Tess, you can do better. You should be ashamed. In fact, I say no bathroom break until you come up with something funny."

Alexa stands. "I second!"

"Me, too," Rory says.

"That's a yes from me." Carrie says.

Leah raises her bottle. "Agree."

Mel grins. "Hell, it's unanimous. Just leave us laughing and you're free to pee."

Now I need to pee and am on the spot. I shift from foot to foot, and I alternate between wiggling and jogging in place. Not an easy accomplishment chock-full of beer and shots.

Mel shakes her head. "The potty dance won't cut it."

"Uh," I wrack my brain. Got it. "Look out, the chains on my mood swing just snapped."

"Ding-ding-ding. Winner!"

Mel speaks into her raised fist. "Rory, tell her what she's won."

Rory sweeps an arm toward the bathroom. "A round trip to the beautiful island of…powder room!"

I bow and dash out of the room. The delay made the urge now urgent. Once relieved, I check myself in the mirror. My lips quiver. "No," I tell my reflection. "He's not crying over you. You are better than this. You'll be fine. You'll be fine. Well, maybe put on some lip gloss and you'll be fine." I obey myself and take a deep breath before opening the door. I also throw out a tissue from on the floor. Pigs.

"Anybody want another?" I shout into the living room as I walk past it and down the hallway to the kitchen. I don't want to re-enter the room without something in my hands. They're still shaky and twitchy.

I don't hear a response or any noise at all from the other room. Also, the girls let me out of their sight for over ten minutes now, which so far has been taboo. This silence is beyond unnatural. The kitchen is ten degrees warmer than the other room where they sit quietly. I am instantly suspicious and sweaty. "Hello? I'm offering alcohol here." No response. Beer feels like a bad idea presently, so I grab a bottle of water from my fridge and search for the mysterious sound of silence. From the edge of the kitchen, I detect hushed gasps and a few, "Oh my Gods."

The previous trickle of sweat now soaks my pits. I stop short and hide behind the half-wall separating the kitchen from the living room. I strain to decipher their conversation, but I can only make out fragments of sentences.

"Well, we don't know for sure, so let's not say anything yet."

The most I hear is one of them says is cryptic. I crouch and inch closer in an awkward duck waddle. I cup my ear and shut my eyes.

"They must be screwing with us. This can't be true."

I believe I hear Rory's voice.

"Yeah, wait for Hannah. Don't rely on what the guys are saying. They could be messing with us."

I clasp a hand over my mouth to stifle my heavy breathing and crawl around the corner for a better view.

They all look down at their phones. Mel and Alexa furiously type away with their thumbs.

No one appears to sense my presence. Despite the heat, a chill travels down the length of my body. I push up from all fours to standing. "What's going on?"

All five of them snap their heads like I'm a teacher who has just returned to the classroom and caught them cheating on an exam. Alexa, Rory, Leah, and Carrie all turn toward Mel as if she's the ringleader.

I sense something is certainly happening despite whatever line of BS they are about to feed me.

"Nuh, nothing, Tess," Mel glances down at the phone and taps. "We're just, just um, catching up on our texts. Yeah, I think we all had our alerts on silent while you were relating the last captivating story." She turns her head. "Right, girls?"

"Yeah, I was just checking my accounts." Leah raises her phone.

Someone's phone pings.

Mel squints at her phone and points to the screen. "Oh look, a new follower."

"How dumb do you think I am?" I hold out my hand, hoping she will give me her phone.

"Sorry, Tess. No can do." She shakes her head and clutches the device to her chest. "How dumb do you think *I* am?"

I know I won't get anywhere with her, so I quickly dive to the couch and seize the phone from Rory's lap. The screen is locked. I enter her birth date but to no avail.

"You, too, Rory? C'mon, what's going on?" I shake the pink-and-green, polka-dotted case in her face.

Rory lunges, snatches her phone, and shoves it down her shirt and into her bra in a fluid swoop. In a booming voice, she alerts the rest of the group to delete and lock. She pinches the bridge of her nose and turns to me. "Trust me, Tess. You shouldn't know. Seriously."

"It was Hannah, right?"

They all nod.

My stomach feels sick, but I must appear calm. I still want them to give me information. "Okay, I trust you. But I also trust you will tell me if something happens I should know. Not that I can fathom anything."

"You got it. Now, should we leave?" Leah asks.

"Yes, I'm ready," I respond even though what I really want is to crawl into bed and forget everything happening. Better yet, I want to stop my mind from picturing the wedding. I psyched myself into partying tonight and looked forward to going by the time the girls arrived, but now I'm scared. I'm afraid of how I'll react outside my comfort zone here.

Alexa shoots a death glare Leah's way.

Leah purses her lips and narrows her eyes. "Oh!"

Mel shakes her head. "Seriously, Leah. Sometimes I think you live on your own planet." She turns to the rest of us. "Actually, guys, I think we should wait a bit longer. Don't you?"

The group mutters words and grunts of agreement.

They all seem hesitant to talk out loud or directly to me. I feel shunned. I think they are suddenly feeling bad for me or know something big. Again, I'm back to scared. "Why?" I move closer to Mel. "Are the male strippers arriving soon?" I put my hands on the back of my head and gyrate my hips. If I don't turn to sarcasm now, I'll resort to despair. I know my limits. In some aspects of my life at least.

"Easy, girl. Rory shot us down." Alexa squeezes my arm. "For the record, I was all for it."

Mel whistles. "Again, Tess, just trust me. Plus, I've got two stories burning holes in my pockets."

"I agree." Carrie offers a wide smile. "Everyone grab a drink. I think we forgot about a couple of epic nights. Leah, please put those waitressing skills to work." She offers the tray of empty shot cups.

"I'm a *server*, thank you very much." She expertly places the tray on her hand palm up, elbow back, and gives an exaggerated bunny-shake before sashaying into the kitchen.

I sink deeply into the couch and snuggle next to Alexa. I can't help trying again. "What did Hannah say?" I whisper.

Alexa pouts. "Don't think about it, Tess. You're doing so well." She points to Leah who has returned with a full tray bearing various cups and bottles. "Looks like you're on again."

"Pick one and get ready to spill." Mel points to the beer in her hand. "Not this drink, but the story of your first legal drink."

Dammit. I should've known crossing my fingers wouldn't be enough to prevent this story from resurfacing. "Oh, God! Do you mean the story of my twenty-first birthday?"

"Start with Adam's the year before since his occurred first."

"You're all cruel." I take a long drag on my beer and point to the bottle. "I know I said I'm sticking to beer since I'm over my shot limit. We'll see if I can hold out after I relive crashing Adam's twenty-first birthday party."

Rory points and peers down her nose. "You might recall we implored you not to go. Repeatedly."

To avoid their stares, I look up at the ceiling.

Mel mimics her younger voice, " 'Tess, don't go. You're just asking for trouble.' I believe were the words I used."

"Hey now." Rory scowls. "I took away your keys."

"Hardly. You're terrible at hiding." I smirk. "Your underwear drawer. C'mon, I hope you never get robbed. You know that is the first place thieves look."

"Oh my God, Rory." Carrie cackles. "You're pathetic. I mean everyone knows that's where you hide the good stuff."

I widen my eyes. "Oh, and there was some good stuff, let me tell you…"

"Please don't," Rory screams and jabs her fingers into her ears.

Leah wrinkles her nose. "Thanks for letting us know where you hide your sex toys, Carrie. Yuck."

"Hey, at least I actually did something to stop her. You guys just told her not to go. Has that ever worked?" Rory asks.

"Tell Tess not to do something, and she'll do it twice and take pictures." Mel winks.

"Enough!" I wave my arms and climb back up on the table. "I went. You know what happened. You already know most of it. Do I have to recount this one? I feel like you're just stalling for some mysterious reason."

"We need to hear the rest of the story. There is always more to your adventures, Tess. If nothing else, tonight has proven that for sure." Mel wags her pointer finger.

I take a deep breath. She's right. Of course, I have more to add. They don't know the whole story. I've only confessed or confirmed bits and pieces, but now, I see no harm in explaining the true sequence of events and details I've purposely omitted.

Adam's twenty-first birthday fell in the fall of my sophomore year at Fairfield. I was still only nineteen due to my spring birthday, but I had a decent fake ID from my older cousin attending UConn. Adam and I had been together the prior summer and hovered in a vague sort of taking-a-break phase as his birthday approached.

Mel points. "Did Adam ever truly ask you to meet them?"

I shake my head. "He never said not to come. Not exactly. During phone calls he repeatedly discussed his birthday, so I felt included."

"It's a wonder you're not a private investigator," Leah mutters and tilts back her red cup.

I ignore her. Adam had been attending Stonehill only thirty minutes from our hometown. I was in Connecticut a couple of hours away. Mid-October seemed like a perfect time to drive up to see him and celebrate the big day. I could also stop at home and do laundry before heading back to school. I thought I conjured a great plan. But I also thought it best not to tell him in advance. I wasn't trying to surprise him exactly, but I was more comfortable not sharing the information. Yes, I was afraid he'd say not to come.

Early Saturday morning, I loaded my car with a full hamper and the summer clothes I planned to leave with my mom. I'd exchange shorts and sandals to return with sweaters, fleece pullovers, and suede boots. The day was sunny and crisp, and I blared a great playlist as I cruised north on I-95. I felt confident, and even though I thought about calling Adam, I didn't want to chance ruining my good mood by possibly waking him before the crack of noon.

I made excellent time, and my mom had lunch waiting. We chatted and ate salads with warm bread while my clothes spun and tumbled down the hall. My dad arrived shortly after his golf game and joined our reunion.

"You must be excited to see Mel and go to the game tonight," Mom said while she cleaned the kitchen.

Lately, she and I were in a good place, and I felt guilty knowing I was visiting under false pretenses, so I was extra chatty. I related tales about tailgating and catching up with my friends who'd be there.

After asking the usual questions about classes, my dad stretched out on the couch to flip between college football games, golf, and dozing.

He was in his happy place, and I knew to let him be. I called my mom the previous Sunday to let her know I was coming home on Saturday. I didn't inform her I'd be spending Saturday night with Adam. Lucky for me, I didn't have to tell her anything, and she just guessed I was going to "the Big Game" at Boston College where Mel attended school.

I called Mel the next day. "In case you see or talk to my mom or anyone who might see or talk to her, could you just play along like I'm coming to hang out with you next weekend?"

"Oh, Tess." Mel sighed. "You know I will. I always cover for you, but this time I don't like it. I know it's his birthday, but I don't think you should go see Adam. I know why you want to go. You think you can prevent him for doing something dumb, but I think you're just asking for trouble."

I should have realized she knew my motive, but I didn't care. I prepared to defend my decision and leapt to my stubborn ways. "Has the possibility of trouble ever stopped me before?"

"Well, if you're going to stir the pot, make sure you have a tight grip on the handle."

"Your Scottish Nana had some great words of wisdom, Mel. Not only do I have a tight grip, I brought my own spoon."

"Can't you just come here and have fun with me instead? I promise you'll have a blast. Even though it's a rare night game, we're planning a huge tailgate starting early with kegs and eggs. And think of the after-party if, I mean, when we win. Say you'll come, and I'll get you a ticket. They've been sold out for weeks, but I think I can snag one more for the student section. I'll even throw in a giant foam finger."

Part of me knew I should accept her proposal. I didn't actually have an invitation from Adam, but I was too afraid of what I'd miss at his celebration. I didn't want to sound unsure of myself, even though I had doubts. "Thanks, your offer is tempting, and I do want a foam finger, but save pulling strings. I might need you to bail me out."

"Not funny. Be smart and have fun, but remember you can always come here."

Mel cringes at my recounting of the momentous day. "You missed the game of the century. Our guys sent those Leprechauns back to Indiana with their heads spinning and their bowl bids flying out the bus windows."

I feel nausea roll. Back then, I thought I knew better, but my friends had my best interests at heart. I should have listened. I've since heard many stories of the fun I missed, and each time I feel the same pit in my stomach as I do now.

"Yes, Mel. I remember the upset of the century. I'm sure I would've had a great time. Yes, going with you would have been the better choice. Yes, I regret not listening to you."

She waits a moment and motions for me to continue.

"You were right, Mel. I was wrong."

"While your apology seems as sincere as a porcupine, I accept it. I just wish you could realize that when you're in a hole, it's time to stop digging."

"Nana?"

"No. This one's from our favorite talk-show doctor."

"Nice. May I continue?"

"It's your shit-show." Mel grins.

I know she's not mad at me. We've never been mad at each other. Sure, we've disagreed, usually about my decision-making skills, and I've been frustrated with her, but nothing ever jeopardized our relationship. She gave up telling me not to go to Adam's and moved on to planning the tailgate for the football game. The pre-game parties were as competitive as the game on the field.

Over the following week, I received calls from Leah, Carrie, and Alexa all warning me not to go, but I was too stubborn. Hannah was studying abroad, but she still managed to call and warn me despite the time difference between Barcelona and New England. I listened and immediately dismissed their advice, thinking I knew better. I also convinced myself into believing Adam would want me there, and everything would be wonderful. I also wondered what would happen in my absence and assumed my presence would prevent any debauchery.

I snort.

After lunch, I told my mom I'd be busy packing some warm clothes and sheepishly padded off to my bedroom, knowing I had bad intentions. I listened for my mom's footsteps while I pulled out a few cardigans and threw them on my bed to look legit. When I thought she was back downstairs, I pulled my door shut and dialed Adam while I flipped through a photo album from high school. "Hey, birthday boy!"

"Hi, Tess. What's up?"

I thought he sounded like he wasn't talking directly into the phone or had me on speaker. Adam knew I hated being put on speaker phone even when he was alone. I told myself he was just busy to explain his lack of enthusiasm upon hearing my voice. "Nothing." I used my flirty voice. "Whatcha doing?"

"Just playing video games with Jeremy now. The

rest of the guys are coming over later."

Ah, so he had the phone wedged between his ear and shoulder so he could hold the controller with both hands. I shook it off. "What's the party plan?"

"Dunno. I'm at their mercy. I assume they'll bring a ton of booze, order pizza, and we'll play some drinking games before hitting the bars."

"Birthday pre-gaming. Cool."

"Yeah. Uh, I hate to be a dick, but I should get back to Jeremy. He bought me the newest auto theft game."

"What a friend." I could picture him staring at the TV screen. I wanted to capture his attention and lowered my voice. "Pause the game for a second. I have something for you, too."

Adam chuckled. "I'll bet you do."

"I have to deliver it in person."

"Cool, we'll have to figure that out later. I kinda gotta go."

Rejection stabbed me. I had to get off the phone before I asked what was wrong or started an argument. "Okay, have fun."

"Thanks. See ya."

Even though I felt my nerves unraveling, I interpreted our exchange to mean I was welcome to join the party. Well, not exactly, but I thought he'd be happy to see me. And he was. At first.

I kissed my parents good-bye, and when they told me to have fun with Mel, I thanked them. I felt a little lump in my throat, but I considered the sensation nerves, not guilt. By the time I parked behind Adam's apartment, my confidence returned. He and a few of the guys he roomed with back in the dorms, plus Ryan, were spending their junior year off-campus in a decent-sized apartment within walking distance from their classes, but more importantly, the bars. I tagged along to move him in back in August. I helped the guys unpack their moms' old dishes and scratched pots and pans while they set up TVs, modems, and game consoles. By midnight, the place looked halfway decent, and I snuck out after pizza and a thank-you hook up.

I knocked on the door and practiced my best smile.

Ryan answered the door in an untucked flannel and baggy khaki shorts. His eyes went wide, then he grinned. "Hey, Tess." He turned on his heels and sang into the apartment, "Adam, someone's here for you." Ryan retreated out of sight without making further eye contact.

Adam's voice echoed from the hallway. "But I thought you said we weren't getting those?" His mouth dropped open, and he stopped walking just short of the doorway. "Oh."

I was dressed for a party in ripped jeans and a tank top, so his attire confused me. A stained T-shirt from high school and basketball shorts? What was I walking into? I tried not to think about what he could've been expecting instead of me.

"Tess?"

"Didn't think I'd miss all the fun, did ya?" I swung my arms around his neck and planted an exaggerated kiss on his cheek.

He didn't say a word.

I feigned a pout and put my hands on my hips. "Where are your manners? Aren't you going to invite me in?"

Adam shook his head. "Yeah, of course." He swept his arm inside the entranceway. "Sorry, it's just that, you know, it's just us guys."

I tossed my car keys on the hall table and followed Adam toward the dark back room. I think it's supposed to be called a great room, but great it was not, and smelly it was. The room reeked of dirty socks, stale beer, and boys. What a stellar combination. I'm surprised no one has invented a candle capturing the essence.

Once my eyes adjusted to the dark room, I scanned the area. About seven guys sat on the mismatched couches, either drinking or playing a video game. I expected to see at least one of the guys' girlfriends or any of the girls who lived across the hall from them last year. "Girls are coming, right? You wouldn't just have a sausage fest for your twenty-first. That's just another Saturday night for you guys."

One of the roommates snickered. Soon, they were all howling.

Only Craig looked at me. "Oh, there will be girls all right. You can bet on that."

He resumed laughing like a twelve-year-old who'd just heard a penis joke.

Adam shifted his weight from foot to foot and did not make eye contact. "You want a beer or something? Pizza and wings are on the way."

I heard his voice quiver just enough for me to know I'd thrown him off.

He finally peeked.

"I'll grab myself a beer." I narrowed my eyebrows, hoping he would get my message to follow me into the kitchen. He didn't appear right away, so I selected a can of budget beer from the fridge and popped it open. My hands shook, and I'd been glad for the prop.

"Standing alone in the guy's grimy kitchen, doubt crept in. I almost texted one of you girls, but then Adam shuffled in, and I recalled my mission. I put my phone back in my pocket and channeled my strength. I took a long swig of their gross beer."

"Strength? You mean your stubbornness," Mel says.

Leah lifts her drink. "Your pigheadedness."

"Yup. I get it." I smirk. "Try obstinacy and broaden your vocabulary."

Leah makes a "W" with her thumbs and forefingers.

I return with an "L" to my forehead.

Mel gives us both the middle finger and tells me to continue with the story.

"So, you're here," he'd said flatly and leaned his back against the sticky, once-white counter.

I wanted to hear him say he wanted me there on his own, so I kept my reply short. "Yup."

"It's just that, I mean, I'm glad but like…" Adam removed his battered and bent baseball hat and ran his hands through his hair. The gesture lifted his shirt. "I don't know what these guys have planned. Might get ugly. You know?"

I stared at his exposed abs and found courage via my attraction. "Has anything ever scared me away before?" I took an exaggerated swig of my beer for show and liquid bravery. I sauntered over and leaned in while placing my hands on the countertop on either side of him, trapping him. "I just want to make sure you have a happy birthday, but if you want me to go, then just say the word." I traced his spine with my right hand and felt him respond against me.

"Now why would I do that?" He leaned down and kissed me.

His kiss felt familiar. I sensed he wanted more of me. I wanted more of him and responded with matched hunger.

My fear he would spend his twenty-first with another girl slipped away. I didn't want the moment to progress to the bedroom, I wanted to drag out the moment and make him glad I came.

The doorbell buzzed. "Pizza!" shouted one of the guys.

The moment was interrupted at a perfect teasing point. I pulled away. "Saved by the bell." I opened the cabinet and pulled out paper plates.

Adam adjusted himself and grabbed a stack of napkins obviously swiped from the donut shop down the street.

I walked beside him into the common room where the guys had paused their video game. It was eerily quiet without the sound of screeching tires and crashing cars.

"Tess is staying," Adam finally announced between bites.

A couple of the guys nodded, and a few grunted.

Ryan stood and faced me. "You've been warned." He laughed and slapped the back of the guy to his left.

I took the words as a dare. "I know what I'm up against." I winked. Two could play at the passive-aggressive game.

Ryan rolled his eyes. "Whatever, Bruh."

When they finished eating, I jumped to my feet to

feel useful. "I'll clean up, you guys." I gathered the paper plates and greasy napkins strewn about the upended milk crates and steamer trunks they used as coffee and end tables. Had I not offered, who knows how long the remains would have fossilized. My cleaning OCD was not in full swing back then, but the constant picking up and straightening signs were present already. Left-out food was a big no-no.

I heard a mumble of thanks, and I left the room to throw away the garbage and wash up in the kitchen sink. I saw dish soap earlier and didn't want to chance what I might find in the bathroom. Attempting to be the gracious guest, I filled my arms with as many beers as I could carry before rejoining the party.

The murmur of voices I heard from the kitchen quieted and ceased altogether as I re-entered the room.

"Thanks, Tess." Adam took a can and popped the top. He then shot a not-so-subtle glance at Tyler, who sat across the room.

I proceeded to pass around the beers while avoiding eye contact with Tyler. I hoped to deter him from whatever warning he planned to deliver.

Tyler cleared his throat and turned to face me. "Uh, Tess, we were just talking again, and you know we like having you around. You're one of the guys and can totally throw down, but I'm not sure you want to be one of us tonight. We can't divulge any more, or it will ruin Adam's surprise."

I ignored the heat creeping up the back of my neck. "Oh, I didn't know it was up to you, Ty." I handed out the last of the cans and turned to face Adam. I licked my lips. "What do you want? It's your birthday."

Adam leaned forward and placed his elbows on his

knees. He removed his hat and gripped the brim between both hands, somehow bending it even more than it already was after years of abuse. His gaze remained downcast on the battered hat. "To be honest, Tess, I don't know what the guys have planned. Seriously, I tried to get them to tell me while you were cleaning. You know I don't want you to leave after coming all this way, but I can't be responsible for what happens tonight." Adam finally lifted his head.

I could see the conflict in the crinkles surrounding his brown eyes. I still felt stubborn and didn't want to leave. I also didn't want to admit defeat in front of his friends. "Deal," I said. "Nothing that happens tonight will ever be used against you." I walked over to the couch, took his nasty hat, placed it on my head, and sat on his lap.

Adam slipped his arms around me. His slight squeeze made me feel he agreed with my decision.

Tyler bent over and deposited his empty beer can on the floor with a hollow thud. "Fine."

"This could get very interesting," Jeremy muttered.

"Drink up! One more beer here, and let's go." another one of the guys had announced.

Leah snorts. "Sounds familiar to tonight."

"Well, I guarantee you we won't be sharing the same experience. At least I hope not. Whenever we do go out."

"We've still got time," Alexa says with a teasing tone. "Go on, Tess. I never heard the whole story, only Carrie's version."

So, then the guys had declared it was time to change and told Adam to make himself presentable. Minutes later, they reemerged wearing button-downs with khakis or clean jeans. We finally left the smelly apartment.

I thought we'd be walking to one of the nicer bars in the neighborhood, but two cabs approached. Apparently, just like with a group of girls, one guy always took charge of ordering the food and cabs. "Where are we headed?" I slid across the pleather seats. The pine air-freshener hanging from the rear-view mirror provided a slight improvement over the smell of burps, farts, and buffalo wings we left behind.

"No clue. I told you," Adam replied, his voice unsteady. "I don't know anything."

Ryan leaned forward. "And we're not telling either. The driver has instructions. He knows where to go and not to say a word, so don't bother."

Adam sighed. "Last chance if you want out, Tess."

"No way. I'm wearing party pants. Now, where are these other girls?"

Tyler, Ryan, and the two other guys in the cab burst out laughing but still refused to acknowledge my question.

Adam just shrugged.

I thought he looked concerned. I know now, years later, he had an inkling of what was about to happen and was more than a little nervous for both of us.

Ten minutes later, Mel texted a photo of the scoreboard from the football game.

Of course, I should've taken it as a sign to jump out. If I had left then, I could've arrived in time for the after-parties in the wake of the epic upset. Instead, I fought motion sickness as the cab crossed the Rhode Island border.

The guys giggled like tweens.

Adam went silent.

I grew suspicious and fidgeted. I felt better when I sensed Adam reaching for my hand in the dark of the cab. His touch thrilled me beyond reasoning. I told myself I would not back down. Even when I had seen the neon blinking sign, I'd told myself I was making the right decision.

I roll my eyes at my naivete. "Another 'sign.' I know, girls." I stand and pace the room. "Here's the thing, I believe everything happens for a reason, but I've learned sometimes the reason is that I'm stupid and make bad decisions."

"Yes." Rory raises her voice. "But remember, good decisions come from experience, and experience often comes from bad decisions."

"And bad decisions make good stories." Leah raises her purple plastic cup. "Continue, I believe you were possibly entering an antique shop?" She squeals at her own joke and hiccups which makes her laugh even harder.

Carrie whacks her on the back. "Never mind her, she's fine. Go on, Tess."

"I had paid my cover charge and nonchalantly offered my hand for a stamp bearing red lips as if I frequented such establishments. I followed the guys through the crowd and ignored the snide remarks from the bouncer, bartender, and random patrons. Yes, I should have left. I knew the night could only go downhill. But, as you all know, I'm stubborn. At that point in my life and in the night, I was downright pig-headed as one of you so nicely mentioned earlier."

I figured I would show Adam and the guys how cool I was by not letting the topless waitresses and dancers bother me. I calmly drank, threw back too many shots, and laughed while the girls pouted and stripped down to G-strings. I even stuffed a few singles of my own to play along. Feigning fun was easy until I lost track of Adam for a while. I tapped Tyler on the shoulder. "Have you seen Adam?"

He cupped his ear and turned his back.

I asked the same question of Chris.

He shook his head but smirked. "Probably taking a leak."

I had a feeling they were covering for him. My chest tightened, but I pushed my way past their protective arms and made my way through the sweaty crowd. Getting pinched and pawed along the way to the back of the club, I saw and heard his friend, Garrett. I like *most* of Adam's friends.

"Woot, woot! Go, buddy!" Garrett fist-pumped the air and ground his hips, yet he stood alone looking into the dark.

I thought he looked foolish, but I was the one who was beginning to feel like a fool. I searched for the object of his cheering in the hazy darkness of the back of the club. I also felt the shots kicking in and the room spinning.

A dancer wearing a superhero get-up straddled Adam. He sat in a chair with his mouth hanging open and his arms dangling by his sides.

From behind the chair, Jeremy held down his shoulders.

I tried to shake it off, but something in me snapped. I think anger was bubbling just below the surface all night, and the scene just made me burst. While I clenched my fists discreetly by my sides, I saw the dancer unhook her gold vinyl bra and shake her silicone-filled boobs in Adam's face.

His eyes were saucers, but he grinned. His hands drifted up toward her and…

Well, I didn't see any more. I guess I reached my boiling point. I bolted.

"To my relief, a line of cabs idled outside. I had opened the door to the closest one and told the driver to step on it."

"Time out. You didn't say those words." Mel shakes her head. "No one actually says that in real life."

I place my right hand over my heart. "I absolutely did."

"Where to?" The cab driver had asked.

"I don't know yet. Where are we?"

The driver laughed. "Just north of Providence."

"Okay, good. Can you take me to Providence College?"

He had banged on the dash meter to reset it. "Yeah, I figured."

Now, I sigh dramatically, step down from the table, and sit on its edge to drain my beer. The girls will know where the story goes from here. For a bit, at least.

"Need a break? Do you want me to pick up from here?" Carrie asks.

She knows the next sequence of events but still not the entirety. I'll let her fill in some details. She earned the privilege. However, I'll wait to elaborate after she tells her part. Tonight feels like the appropriate opportunity to add the epilogue. I nod. "Please." Even privately, I rarely relive this chunk of the night. Recalling makes my chest burn even now.

Carrie remains seated. "I was woken by a knock on

my dorm door around one in the morning."

"She insists 'she has nowhere to go and needs you.' Nicole, my RA, pointed rather disgustedly at Tess. She was a mess of smudged, black eye makeup and ratty hair. She also smelled like, well, a strip club."

"I grabbed her hand and pulled her into my room, 'I'll take care of her. Thanks for understanding, Nikki.' I closed the door quickly before she could advise me of the multiple rules being violated."

"My roommate was back home in Ohio for the weekend so Tess could, and did, sob as loudly as she wanted. She finally passed out on the bottom bunk after I'd hydrated her and stuffed a few ibuprofens down her hoarse throat."

I blow a kiss. "You were a good friend, Carrie." I sigh and pace the floor. "In the morning, Carrie had made strong coffee in her little dorm-sized machine and offered dry, sugary cereal. She even skipped church and drove my sorry ass forty-five minutes to Adam's apartment. I remain eternally grateful." I place my hand over my heart.

Carrie shakes her head now. "Not good enough. I should've stayed the extra minute to watch you drive off. Or not, as it turned out."

"Don't feel bad because I'm an idiot. You'd already gone above and beyond. I would have sped off, too." I turn to the girls. "I'd hugged and thanked Carrie in her car and waved as I walked toward my car. I was grateful to find no parking ticket, then my stomach dropped. The memory of tossing my keys flashed before me."

"Uh-oh." Leah widens her eyes and takes an audible gulp.

"Yeah," I say. "I discovered Rock Bottom has a basement."

I stood frozen in the parking lot and repeated every swear word I knew and created a few new combinations. I contemplated calling my dad to bring the spare set, but I felt the humiliation of facing him would be worse than facing Adam. At least with Adam, I was already embarrassed. I didn't think it could get any more humiliating.

It was almost noon, not early, but early for the morning after your twenty-first birthday party—at a strip club.

I texted him.

I called his cell.

Nothing.

Finally, I just leaned against my car and fiddled with my phone. I checked all my messages twice, trolled social media, and even played solitaire to pass the time. The stench from the apartment's dumpster did nothing to help my hangover. I gagged a few times and walked as far as I could while still visible from Adam's window.

Although I was thankful Indian Summer stuck around another day, I wished I could get into my car and cover myself with a hoodie. My tank looked fine last night. On a Sunday morning, I looked like…well exactly what I was—pathetic.

Ping.

My heart raced and relief washed over me, but the text was from my dad. I cringed. I waited for the second ping and tapped on the avatar—a photo of the two of us at my high school graduation.

—*What a game!*—

170

I replied immediately.

—*I know, right?*—

Then he sent a bunch of emojis he didn't know the hidden meaning of—I hope.

I replied with silly eye rolls and a series of hearts to end the exchange. Fortunately, he prefers texting to actual phone calls, or he would have questioned the concern in my voice. Emojis couldn't reveal my anxiety. Nothing like a smiling pile of poop to mask true feelings.

After what I deemed an appropriate length of time, I dialed Adam's cell again. No answer, but then a movement caught my eye. I looked up just in time to catch a glimpse of a blind swing close. I was sure he saw me, but I waited alone another ten minutes.

The back door of the apartment building squeaked open. Adam emerged wearing a different battered hat than the night before, a sweatshirt from high school, and flannel pajama bottoms with socks and pool slides. He took his time shuffling toward me.

I heard my keys jingle.

He kept his gaze down.

Instead of tossing the keys to me, he held them in an outstretched hand.

I felt the move was deliberate, if not more personal. I stepped closer and allowed my fingers to brush his palm while picking up the keys. "Sorry," I said to break the silence.

"It's okay." He shrugged and lifted his head. "I really don't know what to say about last night."

"You shouldn't have to say anything. You have nothing to apologize for. I made a deal. I knew what I was getting into, sort of." I rolled my eyes to make further light of the situation. "I should have taken the not-so-subtle hints from your friends." I turned toward my car. "I'd better go."

"Wait!"

My heart skipped a beat. I turned back.

"I wanted to find you, but the guys wouldn't let me."

I concealed my smile by looking at the ground. "Ah, I assumed you were pissed, but I hoped just passed out."

"Well, not pissed exactly. Aggravated with you, yeah, but more worried than anything. As for passing out, I guess I must have in the cab. I just woke up and probably will go right back to bed now that I know you're okay."

I shuffled my feet. "I wasn't your responsibility. You didn't have to worry." I lifted my head halfway, just enough to gauge his reaction.

He laughed in a hushed tone. "I'll always worry about you, Tess. You should know that by now."

Relief washed over me, but I still wanted to make sure he didn't hate me. I straightened my spine and faced him fully. "I shouldn't have come. I didn't mean to cause a problem. I just didn't want to be left out."

Adam shook his head. "I get it. You had to see for yourself. I knew you wouldn't retreat. I'm glad you're not mad and you got back okay. The guys took my phone for obvious reasons."

"Gotcha. I went to Carrie's. She took care of me."

"Good. Let's forget about it. Hey, do you want to, um…?" He paused, lifted his hat, and scratched his head. "Never mind, you have a long drive ahead. Be safe."

I thanked him again for understanding and remotely unlocked my doors. I started the engine and backed away, then I glanced in my rearview mirror.

He lingered in the parking lot. I had seen his hangdog expression until I rounded the corner. "I'd like to say I drove straight back to school and got right to work on my psychology term paper. I'd like to say I learned my lesson. I'd like to say a lot of other things I did not do that day."

Mel clears her throat. "Tess, how do you decide each day whether to put on the horns or the halo?"

"Easily. I lost the halo years ago."

Alexa makes an explosion sound. "It spontaneously combusted."

"How can this possibly get worse?" Rory asks. "What did you do, turn around and rush back into his arms?"

"Nope, although God knows I've run back way too many times for you to assume I'd do anything else." I knew I was in the wrong. I had to swallow my pride and just move along.

Rory turns and faces the group. "You know Tess, she never makes the same mistake twice. She makes it five or six times just to be sure."

"Well, for most people, this would be the end of the story. By now you know I'm not like most people. This time I kept driving until I got the bright idea to visit Darcy. You know, while I was in the neighborhood so to speak. Okay, so I had to backtrack a little." I point at my friends now. "Don't search a map app and correct me."

I was already out of the way and wasn't sure of the best route to our hometown, so I'd pulled into a big box store's parking lot to get my bearings. The big red bullseye was a comforting sign, literally. I couldn't wait to use their bathroom and change out of my smelly night-before clothes. Thankfully, I had a trunk full of fall to winter to take back to Fairfield. I rummaged through and found a light, off-white sweater, and soft gray jeans. Score, I thought. I only had my fancy wristlet from the night before instead of my usual, oversized purse, so I carried my clothes into the public restroom. I spent thirty minutes changing, untangling my hair, and washing my face with only water. Then I realized where I was. Big box stores often get a bad rep, but they have everything. I balled up last night's outfit, selected a cart, and proceeded with retail therapy.

By the time I left near two in the afternoon, I was fully made-up and smelled like "lavender mist" body spray. I also tried dry shampoo. Who knew? I got carried away and stocked up on snacks and diet soda for my dorm, too. My debit card got quite a workout. I reminded myself to check the balance on Monday. I pulled out of the parking lot with my car as full as move-in day.

I neared the Powers' house and felt almost normal. I plastered on a smile and rang the doorbell. The familiar chime sounded like home. Even though I had been going there for years, I always rang the bell when I was there to see Darcy.

She loved to answer the door, and I always appreciated her enthusiasm when she pulled me inside. That day, Darcy wasn't expecting me, so I didn't think she'd run for the door as she did on our scheduled Thursdays. I knew her surprised reaction would cheer me.

Mr. Powers opened the door. He wore an apron and held a beer. "Hey, Tess. Come on in. I'm just watching football and making the chili. Mrs. Powers ran out for a couple of last-minute ingredients."

I thought he sounded very casual and not surprised to see me.

Darcy must have heard my voice because she bolted out of her room, sprinted down the hallway, and hopped into my arms.

Her greeting was exactly what I needed to make me feel sane again. I swung her around.

"Well, I'm no longer necessary." Mr. Powers retreated to the family room.

I let Darcy pull me down the hall into her room. We had not seen each other since the end of the summer. She wore a party dress and costume jewelry and spoke fast, yet I didn't sense anything unusual. She showed me her new drawings and described friends at school as she fluttered about her bedroom.

I peered at a painting taped to her wall. She used orange to depict their house and green to represent her parents and Adam. "These are really good, Darcy. I like your color choices."

"You sound funny," Darcy said.

"I was shouting at a football game last night and lost my voice."

She hugged me again. "I hope you find it soon. I like your regular voice."

I assumed she was excited to see me, and I enjoyed the attention. I felt at ease for the first time in days.

"I'm so glad you're here. Mommy didn't think you'd come."

Suddenly I sensed something was going on. I could

hear Mrs. Powers' arrival by the familiar sounds of opening and closing cabinets and the refrigerator like she was putting away groceries. "Sounds like Mommy's home. Let's go see if she needs a hand." I made the suggestion more out of curiosity than altruism.

Darcy loves to help and skipped into the kitchen. "She did come, Mommy! I told you Tessie would come."

She turned toward me with a wide smile. "Tess, what a nice surprise."

"Actually, I was just in the area. I went to the big BC game last night and was heading back to Connecticut. Thought I'd stop in and see my favorite girl." I patted Darcy's head.

"Oh, Tess. It's okay. I told Adam to ask you to join us if things were, you know, good between you two. I never know and hate to ask, but I hope you both know you are always welcome here." She tilted her head toward the wall clock above the arched doorway. "He should be here soon."

Shit. My stomach flip-flopped. He was coming home for his birthday dinner. Birthday chili. How did I miss the connection? Chili was his dinner choice every year. Now I was stuck. Should I cover or tell the truth? Whose feelings were the most at risk? Mine were already decimated. "Uh, yeah. Of course. You know, it's always kinda weird." I hoped to sound light and unconcerned. The opposite of how I felt.

"I suppose weird is as good as any word to describe you two."

Darcy tugged on my sweater. "Wanna see the cake?"

Mrs. Powers flashed a smile and announced she was wrapping gifts in her room.

Darcy opened the fridge to reveal a homemade cake she had obviously frosted. The writing was adorably messy.

I choked up. Then I heard Adam announce his arrival, and I felt the tender moment break.

Darcy squealed and ran out of the kitchen.

I didn't know where to go so I just stayed put and gripped the back of an oak kitchen chair. He surely saw my car parked out front.

After an eternal and uncomfortable amount of time alone, I finally spied Adam. My shoulders relaxed, but I kept my jaw clenched.

He inched into the kitchen and halted in the doorway. Adam leaned against the curve of the entryway arch and grinned. He'd showered, shaved, and upgraded from pajama bottoms.

I could smell his shampoo. I loved that smell and the way his jeans fit and…I almost forgot the last twenty-four hours. I snapped back and remembered I was the one who needed to explain. I held up both of my hands. "This is not what you think. I had no idea you were coming home. I probably should have, but I honestly planned to just visit Darcy to cheer up myself before heading back to school. Your parents assumed I came for your party. I panicked and didn't correct them. I'm truly sorry."

He laughed. "Don't apologize. I like when you're here. I should have asked you a while ago, and the only reason I didn't invite you today when I had the chance was because I felt bad asking you to drive all this way." He shuffled closer to the table but stopped short of touching distance.

"Thanks, Adam. For being so cool about this." I smiled and moved in closer. Thankful I'd taken advantage of a perfume sample at the store, I placed both hands on his chest. I could feel his heart thump beneath my hand, and my confidence returned. "So, did you have a good time?"

He reached around my waist and pulled me into a hug. "Listen, I don't really like, ever, want to talk about last night again. It was pretty gross." He looked down and grinned.

"All my anxiety from the entire weekend slipped away while we had embraced." A flush burned my cheeks.

"Oh, God." Alexa rolls her eyes. "Was this the beginning of another short-lived bout of dating?"

"Not exactly…"

"No! Wait a minute." Rory holds up her right hand and points with her left. "Don't tell me this is the time you guys hooked up in the basement while everyone was upstairs, including his grandparents?"

"I needed to give him his birthday present." I wince and take a sip of my beer.

Leah punches my arm. "You've got to be kidding."

"That's truly disgusting." Mel giggles.

I cross my arms over my chest. "That's not how I remember it."

While couch pillows are launched, I laugh along with their cries of "Eew" and "Yuck." I bat the projectiles and laugh at myself and enjoy the momentary reprieve from tears. I pick up the cushions. "All right, I've had enough. Let's get out of here."

Mel exchanges a glance with Alexa.

A phone pings.

"Did one of you just text the other?" I ask.

Ping.

"No," they both snap.

"How about one more story?" Mel asks.

I think she answers too quickly.

"Good idea," Alexa says.

"How about I make an announcement unless you tell me what you're discussing?" I glare at Alexa. "I can easily change tonight's guest of honor."

Mel tilts her head. "What?"

"Nothing." Alexa stares. "There is nothing to tell."

I scowl. "Yet."

"Okay, cut whatever shit is going on between you two." Mel sighs. "Tess, you just need to trust us. We can't leave right now."

"Somebody roast Adam or Tess or both stat," orders Alexa.

"Ooh, ooh I got one. I got one!" A very buzzed Rory hops up on the table.

Mel climbs up too and whispers in Rory's ear.

I think I hear Mel tell her to make the story last a long time.

Rory and Mel exchange whisper positions. Rory murmurs something behind a cupped hand.

Even though I can't hear the words, whatever she said makes Mel don an evil grin.

"Grab a drink from the kitchen, ladies." Mel circles an arm.

Rory points. "Be good while we're gone." She stumbles to the floor.

I cross my heart, but as soon as everyone leaves the room, I search the couch and floor for a neglected phone. My efforts are futile since no one was dumb enough to leave an unprotected device behind.

Thankfully, I've hit the comfortably numb stage, and Adam's wedding feels more like fiction. Despite the occasional humiliation, I enjoy reliving our stories. At this point, I feel confident the worst is over and allow myself to daydream about some of the memories shared tonight while I wait for the girls to return and resume my roast.

Rory reclaims her perch on the coffee table. "Tess blew Adam's good time at his party." She pauses and snorts. "But he got his turn to cock-block on Tess's twenty-first." She curtsies and steps down.

I breathe deeply and ready myself to relive the night I ruined my chance of marrying a doctor.

Chapter Twelve

"Oh, right." Alexa sinks into the couch. "Remember Ian?"

Rory nods and twists the top of a water bottle. The cap makes a loud crack. "He was too good to be true."

"Too good for the likes of me, you mean." I point at Rory and wink. The gesture is getting more difficult to perform.

"No." She points back and waggles her finger. "He was just a good guy, which at the time couldn't hold a candle to your bad boy."

"Unfortunately, I agree. I let him slip away."

Leah stands and adjusts her cropped top. "Uh, more like you ran him off, screaming all the way." She windmills her arms, sending her shirt up her chest.

Carrie leans over and yanks down the shirt with a loud, "Hmpf!"

"Good work, Care, and thanks, Leah. For the record, I ran him off, but he was not a screamer." I stick out my tongue. "Truth is, I don't know for sure. I never did, um, you know, go there."

"You're despicable," Mel lisps.

Her impression is spot on, with the aid of alcohol.

"Hey, last I checked this was a roast, not a lovefest." I throw back my shoulders.

"She might need the lovin' later." Rory stands and squeezes me while steering me back onto the table.

"But for now, let's set our minds back to Tess's twenty-first birthday. I'd like to say that was the night of her first alcoholic beverage, but I'd also like to say I'm a size zero, and we all know both are lies."

I smack Rory on the ass and take my perch with a lot less grace than I did just a few hours and drinks ago. During my junior year at Fairfield, I'd spotted a new guy. I noticed him right away in my Psychology III seminar. I was certain I'd never seen him on campus before.

He sat directly in the middle of the auditorium while I preferred the aisle toward the back. He always lingered after class, furiously writing on a legal pad, not a standard spiral notebook, or even a tablet or laptop like everyone else.

I'd been licking my wounds from the most recent after-summer break-up with Adam, and I simply enjoyed the view for the entire month of September. By October, I became too curious and approached him after a Tuesday lecture. I took advantage of the fact he was still sitting, capping his pen and yellow highlighter. I attempted to sound friendly, but not bubbly or fake like I witnessed so many girls do when approaching a cute guy. I chose short and sweet. "Hey."

"Hi." He pocketed his pen without looking up.

When he did see me, he smiled with his whole face. With his sandy hair, light blue eyes, and generous freckles, he was already the opposite of Adam. "I'm Tess. I was wondering if you're new here since it's the third year of Psych, and I recognize most of the other students in this class from prerequisites."

"Yeah, you guessed it. I am new. Nice to meet you, Tess. My name's Ian, and I just transferred in from

Santa Clara." He stuck out his hand.

I shook his hand and lingered before dropping my arm and cocking my head. I felt my eyebrows narrow.

He laughed softly. "I get that reaction a lot. You want to know why I'd leave sunny California for east coast winters, right?"

"No, actually." I relaxed my face and scanned my thoughts for a unique and witty remark to challenge the stereotype he might be forming. I also wanted to stand out from any other girls who had already asked the predictable question. "I want to know why you've been here six weeks already and haven't asked me to get coffee?"

He grinned and blushed simultaneously.

Heat crept up my neck, and my stomach fluttered. Was I flirting? Was he responding?

He gathered his books, stood, and offered an arm. "Please accept my sincere apologies, Tess. I would've asked you for coffee the first day I noticed you over there on the aisle, but I assumed a gorgeous girl like you would have a huge, muscle-clad boyfriend who would kick my ass."

Uh-oh, I thought. This could be dangerous. I enjoyed the easy banter I'd yet to find with any other boy on or off campus. I couldn't help myself. "I can assure you there will be no ass-kicking."

"Because he's at the gym now, pumping up to pound me later?"

Don't think about Adam, don't think about Adam. I repeated the mantra silently while I walked beside this gentleman. "Because he doesn't exist. Now, unless you have another class to get to or a needy, insecure girlfriend for me to intimidate, let's go to the café across the street."

Over coffee, I learned Ian was from a nearby town in Connecticut. He transferred to be closer to his family since his father was recently diagnosed with a recurrence of stomach cancer. His family insisted he stay out west, but he couldn't bear the distance and made all the arrangements on his own.

I understood and nodded. "I'm an only child, so I get it. My dad and I are close. This is as far as I am willing to go away from home." I tried not to think—or from Adam, which made me think about Adam more—so I swayed the conversation by asking Ian about himself.

He was pre-med and taking a huge course load and hoped I didn't mind if we walked back to the main campus so he could get a couple of hours in at the library before his evening class.

"Is this your schedule on Thursday, too?"

He held the café door. "Yes. Did I pass?"

I walked out to the sidewalk and paused.

He kept his gaze forward. "If so, would you like to do this again?"

I chuckled. "I think I can elevate to lunch since you passed. I didn't realize you had such a long day. My classes are morning loaded. I'm done for the day." I walked with him to the library. I chatted easily and felt comfortable offering my number before leaving the granite entrance steps. Sporting a goofy smile the whole way, I walked back to my dorm.

As soon as I walked into our room, Rory sauntered over. "What have you been smoking?"

"I met a boy," I said in a little kid's voice.

"Thank God." Rory hugged me so hard she picked

me up off the floor. "I've been waiting for this moment."

I knew Rory was dying to set me up, but she knew I'd never go for it. Finding someone had to happen on my own terms. I just never knew what those terms would be. Psychology class sure wasn't what I envisioned. I still couldn't believe I developed strong feelings so quickly and was shocked to find my thoughts wandering to picturing my life as a doctor's wife.

On Thursday, I sat in my usual seat and met Ian in the hall after class. Lunch was as relaxed as coffee, and I felt a calm I never experienced with another guy. I filled him in on my courses and plans to pursue physical therapy. I was searching for an internship and thought I sounded like I had my act together. When I mentioned a few upcoming parties, though, I realized my priorities didn't align with his.

Ian planned to study all weekend. He claimed he was still catching up in some of his classes due to the transfer. I later learned he had no subjects to catch up in, only excel at, and he was too humble to show his inner genius right away.

After a weekend of my usual debauchery, I pulled the old stay-up-talking-too-late-and-not-starting-any-homework-until-Sunday routine. I thought about him several times and considered sending a quick text, but I decided to avoid rocking the boat and to wait until Tuesday's class to pick up where we left off.

His call at noon surprised me. I'd yet to crack a book.

"I was wondering if you'd like to meet for a late dinner tonight. I have a tough week ahead and could use a break."

I was more than happy to have a good excuse to prolong the Sunday all-nighter I usually pulled to finish my reading. At eight, I met him at the local mediocre burger, pizza, sad-attempt-at-salad place. The conversation was effortless, and I enjoyed getting to know someone new for the first time in a long time. At nine-thirty I followed him outside, and I thought we'd catch the campus bus or a cab back, but he pointed toward a blue sedan.

"Oh, I forgot to mention, I'm living at home and commuting to campus each day." Ian shrugged. "It's not so bad."

He didn't appear to want my sympathy, so I didn't offer any and searched for something else to talk about. I slid into the passenger's seat. As the engine started, the console lit up. I found my diversion. "The true compatibility test." I pointed to his radio. "What station were you listening to or CD were you playing?"

He blushed. "Yikes. I don't remember!"

Thankfully, it was a sports talk station, and he laughed when he shared he'd been listening to the Red Sox who were in the playoffs.

I turn to Rory. "Remember that? I was immediately flattered and shocked. No way would Adam ever abandon a playoff game for me."

"Adam?" Rory pipes in. "Try no other guy ever! Ian was other-worldly."

I sigh. "I know. I still feel bad."

"You never talk about him." Rory tilts her head. "I've always wondered if it's because you forgot all about him or feel guilty."

"My vote is guilty," Carrie says.

I slouch. "I screwed up. Yes, so of course I feel bad and don't like reliving the mistake I made. Were we right for each other? Probably not. I was smitten by the attention, but clearly, that wasn't enough. Ugh. Do I really have to re-tell this?"

"Continue." Alexa nods. "Confessing is a vital part of your therapy."

"He'd driven the short distance to my dorm and parked at the side door. He turned down the radio's volume and cleared his throat."

For the first time, I grew uncomfortable in his presence. My neck warmed, and my hands shook. I imagined him saying we should just be friends. "Then he politely asked if he could kiss me." He asked! I nodded and leaned in for a sweet kiss which easily could have been a scene from a rom-com movie. He even thanked me after he pulled back and smiled.

"On Tuesday, I arrived in the lecture hall and spied him sitting in the back row. A faded denim jacket draped over the seat beside him. My seat. It remained my seat, and we met for lunch on Tuesdays and Thursdays until my birthday in April, as Pysch III was a two-semester course. Ian occasionally accompanied me to campus parties, but mostly our dates were simple, private dinners, lunches, and movies. Sometimes we'd hook up in my room, but he never stayed over. He never invited me to his house. He was my on-campus boyfriend."

"Therefore, you were free to sleep with Adam over Christmas break?" Mel blurts.

I shoot her a dirty look. "Hey, you still hang around me and watch everything I do—that makes you a fan, bitch." I smile and turn back to my audience.

"Ian was sweet, studious, and polite. An all-around great guy," Rory says.

"He truly was. He probably says the opposite about me."

"Poor Ian, if he'd only known early on your standards were much lower," Rory says. "I remember when he texted me to meet him to plan your surprise birthday party. I couldn't believe how much thought he'd put into the details. And he didn't even plan to attend. He wanted a special girls' night for you and all of us. I mean, can you get any kinder?"

"I know, I know." I stick my fingers in my ears. "Enough, you guys. You're right, but remember what I also explained about our time together?"

"It was perfect?" Leah asks.

I drop my arms. "No. I told you guys, we had a mature, sweet relationship filled with lunch and dinner dates, walks, and movies. I felt appreciated and special, but there was no…"

"Drama?"

I point to Alexa with my beer bottle. "Yes, for sure no drama. But no excitement either. Our relationship was kind of boring. At the time, I told myself boring was exactly what I needed. All of you told me the same, but a few of you confessed it would only be a matter of time before I tired of Ian." Maybe I would've tired of him eventually. Maybe I'd be married to a surgeon on staff at Mass General by now. We'll never know because I screwed up.

"Let's remember Adam is not entirely innocent in this situation," Leah says.

"Or ever," Mel mutters into her beer bottle.

I wave around the room. "I know some of you

188

think I tipped off Adam, but I assure you I did not. I was having a great time with all of you, thanks to Ian. I did not make the booty call. To this day I still believe someone saw us and texted him." I look around the room to see if anyone will fess up.

Mel puts a hand over her mouth then lifts her chin slightly. "Ryan." She dashes out of the room.

I gasp, jump off the table with a thud, and run after her. She beats me to Alexa's room and slams the door. I hear the harsh click of the lock. "Get out here, coward. You can't drop a grenade and just run away."

"Ha Ha! Watch me," says Mel via the courage of her many drinks and the security of a locked door.

I sigh. I know from past experiences she's torn between wanting to sound tough and spilling the beans. Alcohol is on my side for bean spilling. "Hannah's not here, Mel. You can tell me. You know you want to."

She opens the door, just enough for her face to partially peek out.

I resist pinching and twisting her nose.

"She didn't do it intentionally," Mel says.

"Oh, okay. Like she just texted our whereabouts to Ryan by accident. I'm sure that happens all the time."

"No, not exactly. She posted a selfie from the dueling piano bar. Ryan and Adam were together, and Ryan showed him."

Behind the stage hung a huge sign of a moon with two wolves howling at each other in the shadow. The location was unmistakable. I narrow my eyes. "And they drove an hour and a half from Stonehill once they saw the post?"

Mel steps out of the bedroom. "No, they suspected something would happen, so they surprised Ryan's brother, Matt, at UConn. They were already in Hartford at another bar when they saw the post and only had to cab over."

"Damn, Adam never told me how he knew where I was. Part of me wondered why I didn't hear from him that day, but I just figured he'd call the next day on my actual birthday. I never brought up that night again."

Leah walks over and puts an arm around my shoulders. "One of those other girls we don't see anymore told him about Ian and the plans. She had no idea what she was saying or who she was saying it to. By the time I got the information to warn you, the damage was done."

"Thanks, Leah. I wasn't aware, and thanks for trying. Ian and I never talked about the night again either. I'm still ashamed. He went to so much work and expense. Ian deserved better." All these years later, my face burns with shame.

I sulk back to the living room, and Mel doesn't follow me. I near the room and can hear the tapping of her texting, but I know they won't tell me anything. I'm getting suspicious now, but I lose myself back in the memory.

Ian had arranged for the perfect girls' night out. He'd met Rory at a campus cafeteria to discuss the guest list. He then emailed her, Mel, Hannah, Carrie, Leah, and Alexa, plus a few other girls who I was close with back then.

Rory was instructed to get me to a restaurant nearby for a drink and appetizers.

After a drink, and chips and guac at the bar, I assumed we'd sit for dinner.

But the hostess approached and apologized.

I was told no table was available, but to follow her outside. I was confused until I reached the sidewalk, where a stretch limousine was parked. I immediately knew Ian was behind the whole thing. In the limo were pizzas from my favorite place, champagne, and good beer.

While popping the cork, Rory told me how he set up the whole thing and spared no details.

During the ride, I video chatted him from my phone with a flute of champagne in hand.

He appeared on screen with a smirk. "Having fun, birthday girl?"

I blew a kiss. "This is amazing! You are the best boyfriend ever! This is the nicest thing anyone has ever done for me."

He blushed and looked away from the screen.

I deduced from the background décor he sat in his bedroom. Not that I'd ever been there, but I could tell. Where else would one display his debate team trophies?

"You deserve it." He smiled and waved at the screen. "Have a great night."

"Ian, I wish you were here." I held up my glass of champagne and toasted him. "Where are we going, by the way?"

He made the zipped lips gesture. "It's a surprise. Just enjoy the evening."

"Thank you." I felt like I should've told him I loved him, but we weren't declaring that sentiment. I believe he attempted once before but held back. The words scared me, too, since I'd never said them to anyone except Adam. I decided in front of my friends wasn't the best place either. In hindsight, I'm so glad I didn't.

After I consumed three drinks, the limo pulled up to the awninged entrance of a dueling piano bar in Hartford. Rory told me Ian had researched the venue for weeks and even sent a playlist of my favorites ahead to the manager.

I'd never been to one before, but I was a sucker for—and sucked at—karaoke. This was like karaoke on steroids with a much better dressed and talented crowd.

Carrie bought our first round of drinks, something sweet and oh-so Carrie. The syrupy liquid went down fast and packed a punch. I shed my light sweater revealing a sparkly tank top. After several glasses of limousine champagne and a shot at the restaurant, I was singing at the top of my lungs. I remember the photos safely stashed away in the shoebox in my bedroom closet. I was arm in arm with Hannah and Mel, singing a pop song from our high school years.

While belting out a party anthem, I spied Adam in the crowd. I was on stage, of course. I saw him throw back a shot. I think I had a beer in each hand, and before I knew what was happening, we were singing a duet, and my friends were prying me off him.

Mel returns.

I pause my recounting.

She sits on the edge of the couch and stares at her feet.

I could drill her, but instead, I address the whole group. "Okay, confession time. Who else knew Adam was coming to the bar?"

Leah raises a hand. "I know the answer."

I point like a teacher calling on a student. "Yes, Leah?"

"Hannah got a text from Ryan warning her they

were on their way."

I'm truly shocked I didn't figure this out before. "And Hannah didn't think to tell me?"

"She said she tried, but you were performing, and we all know what you're like when you're in the zone. Also, I think she wanted to see Ryan."

"Right." Carrie nods several times. "We lost track of those two for a little while that night also."

I shoot glares at the girls. "And nobody tried to stop what happened next?"

Alexa looks up at the ceiling.

A sound like a weak whistle cuts the silence.

Mel sighs. "Honestly, Tess, would it have made a difference?"

I shrug. "No. Probably not."

In the limo, Adam had reciprocated the birthday favor I gave him the year before.

I am pond scum. I felt like it, too, the next morning. I'm sure I looked as green as I felt when I met Ian for our previously scheduled brunch. Adam rode back to campus in the limo with us, and he subsequently passed out in my narrow, university-issued, twin bed. I had to climb over Adam to meet my boyfriend—my sweet, too-good-for-me boyfriend.

At the café, I attempted to pass off my deplorable appearance and attitude on my hangover. Ian didn't say I looked fine, and his usual smile was replaced with a tight-lipped grimace. I guessed he expected me to gush about the evening. I should have and would have, but I feared revealing any incriminating evidence. I didn't linger over coffee or get a refill. Neither of us even bothered with excuses about having lots of homework.

When I got back to my stuffy, stale room, Rory

was in our kitchenette, and Adam had moved to the pleather couch we inherited from Rory's parents. He was lying on his stomach with his right arm and leg hanging over the edge, and his hat covered his face. It didn't quite hide his drooling. "I don't deserve Ian," I'd told Rory and pointed at Adam. "I deserve that."

"I didn't end the relationship with Ian right away. I was too much of a coward. I met him for a few more lunches where he spoke less and less and only about classes and the weather. Two weeks later, he'd moved to the middle of the auditorium and didn't save a nearby seat."

"You never spoke again?"

I grit my teeth. "I'm such a shit. I avoided him the last few weeks of the semester. I went to class late, left early, and dodged the places I knew he frequented between classes."

"Did you ever run into him during your senior year?" Carrie asks. "I mean, it's not that big of a school."

I sneak a side-eye glance at Rory.

"Go ahead, tell them," Rory says. "No reason to hold back now."

I cover my eyes. "It's so humiliating…"

Leah wiggles in her seat. "This should be good."

"Ugh, ok. I dodged him the entire first month of senior year, but in October, after a very sloppy evening, apparently, I called him super late."

Leah raises her eyebrows. "Apparently?"

"The next day I saw a notification on my phone, a missed call from Ian at 3:23 am. I panicked, wondering why he called at such a crazy time. I checked my call history and sure enough, I had called him at 2:30, and that call ended at 3:22. So whatever I said for almost an hour prompted him to call back, and I didn't answer. I had zero recollection of any call."

"Please tell me you called him back," Mel yells.

"Sorta." I pause and look away. "I texted."

"You wimp."

"Yup."

—*Hi, sorry about whatever I called about last night. I guess I was kinda drunk.*—

He replied an hour later.

—*No worry, so long as you are okay. I called back cuz you just went silent and wanted to make sure you were all right. Assume you just fell asleep.*—

—*Yeah, probs passed out. Sorry again. Um, was I talking nonsense? Give away all my deep dark secrets? Hopefully, apologized for being a jerk last year?*—

Ian replied right away.

—*Nothing to worry about, but if you don't remember, let's leave it like that.*—

—*Yikes, that bad?*—

—*No, just trust me you'd rather not rehash it.*—

—*I'm sorry, Ian. For more than whatever I said last night.*—

—*It's okay*—

—*No, I'm really sorry.*—

—*I wish you all the best, Tess. Gotta go.*—

—*I hope you find someone wonderful.*—

He replied with a smiley face emoji.

"Wow, heavy." Alexa widens her eyes.

"I know. What's worse is all the horrible things I think I might have said for over an hour." I cover my face with both hands. "The humiliation is my punishment."

"No wonder you don't talk about it," Carrie says. "We won't either anymore."

I hear a heavy sigh followed by a throat-clearing cough.

"I recently researched him on social media," Leah whispers.

I lower my hands. "Don't be ashamed." I chuckle. "So did I."

"Me, too," Rory says. "Anyone else?"

Four hands shoot upward.

"He looked good. Didn't he?" I swig my beer. "Go ahead. Just say it."

"Damn, he looked fine!" Carrie shakes her head.

The rest of the girls nod.

"Maybe it's time I make another late-night call." I wink.

Chapter Thirteen

"Ahem! It's called Karma, and it's pronounced, Ha-ha-f-u. I heard that one months ago, and I have been waiting for the right moment to bust it out."

Leah snickers and slaps her thigh.

No one responds.

She's still laughing, and the surrounding silence makes me uncomfortable. "Well, if you can't say something nice...make it funny."

Mel nods. "Or crude."

Rory shakes her head. "Leah, God gave you a good heart, but somebody from the South gave you that mouth."

"Yeah, from way south—like Hell."

The familiar banter puts me at ease, and I lean back in my seat and unclench my hands, now sweaty from the Ian recounting. I wipe them on my jeans. Since I'm already being gross, I sniff my pits. Not exactly fresh, but they could be worse. I'll spritz some body spray before leaving.

Alexa stands and adjusts her outfit. She pulls down the legs of her jeggings and pulls up her plunging neckline. Maybe she'll let it slip later, but for now, she doesn't need to waste her cleavage on us. Instead of stepping up onto the table to deliver another roast as I expect, she walks around to the back of the sofa and disappears for a moment. A rustling ensues, and Alexa pops back up, revealing several black-and-white, chevron-striped gift bags. All the bags are identical, but each has different, brightly colored tissue paper sprouting from the top.

"Nice presentation," I say. "Which blog?"

"Shush, you." Alexa admonishes me with a scowl before turning back to the girls. She shakes the bags to get everyone's attention. The rustling ceases the chatter. "Now, if I remember correctly, this is supposed to be a party, and what's a party without presents?" she sing-songs.

"Just a meeting!" Leah turns to kneel backward on the couch and reaches to grab a bag from Alexa.

Alexa pulls it away and slaps Leah's hand.

Leah dons a hang-dog expression.

"Down, girl. You know the rules." Alexa raises the bags. "So, this will be like a Yankee swap, but nastier."

"Yes!" I fist-pump the air. I love swaps. I started the tradition amongst our friends at Christmas when we were thirteen, and the theme was hair accessories. Over the years, we've done a million exchanges. I am a master at manipulating the trade to end up with the gift I want most. For a minute, I'm genuinely excited, then I remember to relax and channel my poker face. I fear something else must be up since they all know my tricks in this game. However, they appear stoic and seem confident by the looks of their smug grins. They are out to get me. I can only imagine what nastiness could be hiding under the cover of coordinating bags. I cringe remembering the "toys" I saw in the store on Route 1.

Alexa nods to Carrie who then tiptoes over to Alexa and selects a bag with pink tissue paper.

She delivers it delicately as if filled with breakable crystal.

"Open yours first, Tess." Carrie remains standing in front of me with clasped hands until she is pulled down to the couch.

By their silence, I sense a collective anxiety, and my heart races. I like to torture them. I dangle the bag and shake it. "Now?"

"Yes, now!" Rory replies.

I clutch the bag to my chest. "Are you sure this one is for me?"

Leah groans. "For crap's sake, Tess. Open it or I will."

I dig through the bag and create loud crinkle sounds. "Ta-da!" I pull out a thin, white tank with the words *Hot Mess* written in black script. I love it instantly. I know I can't show how much I want the shirt for fear of being swiped. "Cool." I gently smooth the shirt over my legs even though I want to try it on.

"Alrighty, I'm next," Rory practically screams.

She gets louder with every drink, and her current volume reflects a six-pack and countless shots.

Rory leans over and selects a bag from the coffee table. The canary yellow paper flies around her head while she rummages. She peeks inside then whips out something black.

"Ha-ha. I see your hot mess and raise you a walking disaster." She wriggles her eyebrows and swipes the tank from my lap. As she turns to walk away, she tosses the black T-shirt over her shoulder like a piece of trash.

I catch the shirt in mid-air and raise it to view the gold lettering. I sneer. "Even better," I say through clenched teeth.

The *Walking Disaster* shirt is cool. I would totally wear it. But I want the *Hot Mess,* too. I can picture myself strutting into the gym sporting either shirt. I just hope the next bag doesn't contain a plaid flannel or ugly novelty sweater. I don't want to end up with cat pajamas. Anything is possible. One year, the organizer limited our Christmas swap to TV commercial items. I got a pocket-sized garden hose. Everyone thought I got a bum deal, but I have been using the gift to my advantage. Sometimes, I smuggle it into bars. The pun possibilities are endless.

"Next!" Alexa points to Mel.

With much rustling, Mel slowly opens her bag and reveals the back of a black tank. She stands, hesitates, and slowly rotates the shirt to show the wording centered on the chest area. *Caution: Contents Contain Alcohol.* She struts, sporting a shit-eating grin, and pulls the tank over my head.

I stick my arms through the holes and relinquish the *Walking Disaster* shirt. So far, I want them all. Deciding will be tough. Maybe that's the catch. I can only hope it's nothing worse.

Carrie giggles. "I can't wait any longer." She throws the tissue paper. The bag tears in her effort to pull out a white T-shirt. Purple tissue floats to the floor, and she squints to read the message. "Drinks Well With Others."

"Oh, that I do!" I reach over and snatch the new T-shirt. In one fluid motion, I lift the *Caution* shirt over my head and fling it into Carrie's lap.

Leah holds her bag above her head. She bounces in her seat. She turns to Alexa and gestures back and forth.

"Me or you?"

Mel rolls her eyes and sighs.

"Go ahead, Leah," Alexa says. "I'll open last since no one wants to witness your temper tantrum. I can wait my turn. You know, like a grown-up."

"Yay!" Leah ignores the insult and claps rapidly. She rips open her bag and tosses the turquoise paper. She pops up from her seat and parades around the room holding a black, sleeveless T-shirt adorned with sparkly print. *Classy, Sassy, Bad Assy*. The words are stacked, and the first two are crossed out. She makes an exaggerated show of sashaying close. "I hate to part with this, but…"

I toss the *Drinks Well* shirt.

Leah catches it in mid-air.

She hands me the black T-shirt as if she's presenting a crown on a velvet pillow. "Thank you, kind subject." I pat Leah's head.

"That just leaves me." Alexa points toward Leah.

Leah delivers the last bag on her way back to the couch.

Alexa coughs several times, removes the lime green tissue, and pulls out a white T-shirt bearing hot pink, block lettering. *#Status Update: Available*. She forces a smile.

I wonder if she's testing to see if I think the slogan is funny or sad.

I feel all the girls' attention on me. I read it again and absorb the meaning and finally—the reality. The urge to burst out laughing and bawl hit me at the same time.

"Wait, Tess. Look at the back."

Alexa turns the shirt revealing the back: "*You bring*

the alcohol. I'll bring the bad decisions."

Rory squeals and claps. "We added that ourselves."

I clutch my sides and repeat the phrase through spurts of laughter. I slip off the couch and land on the floor by Mel's feet.

Mel nudges me with her bare toe. "Well, Tess, that was the last gift. You know how this works. Your choice. But this time, we'll pick numbers to see who gets to steal."

I hoist myself back onto the couch and consider my options. I believe the secret is to pick my second favorite and hope no one selects my first choice. Since I get the last number, I stand a chance of pulling a good number. I casually select *Hot Mess*.

Mel passes around a miniature shopping bag filled with small slips of paper.

Leah picks a slip first, peeks at the paper, and refolds it quickly before passing along the bag.

Each girl takes a number and averts her gaze.

The bag finally lands in my lap. The last slip of paper sits at the bottom, folded multiple times. All their eyes are downcast, and I wonder why they are avoiding me this time. I hear a stifled giggle. I fumble to unfold my slip of paper. Instead of the number I expected to find, I see a full sentence. *Surprise! They're all for you. Who else is a hot mess of a walking disaster who drinks well with others, is sassy, bad-assy, full of alcohol, and available?*

"You dogs." I jump to my feet and hug each friend separately. I'm psyched and feel like crying at the same time. I didn't see this coming at all. They've never pulled a prank on me, and this was a good one. "Let's get a selfie with everyone holding a shirt."

"For posterity only," Alexa warns. "You know the deal—no posting anything on social media tonight."

I cross my heart and don my best selfie smile. I smoosh between Rory and Alexa, then I swap positions for various shots. I appreciate how lucky I am to have the love and support of these girls. I only hope I'm half as good a friend in their times of need as they've been to me. I still want to punch all of them. "These are awesome, you guys. But you should have gifts, too. I wish I had thought of it." I'm truly disappointed in myself and must find fabulous thank-you gifts next week after the dust settles on this mess.

Had my mother known about this "party" tonight, she would have searched "fun favors for girls' night party" and forwarded me links. I can just see the monogrammed compacts and painted wine glasses now.

Alexa smiles and wraps her arm around my shoulders. "Don't worry about us. Lucky for you, we're selfish."

"Yeah, relax. Mel got us all tanks; she couldn't resist. And I couldn't wait." Carrie lifts her loose halter top and reveals a tight ribbed tank with *TEAM TESS* emblazoned in gold across the chest.

The writing appears familiar. The tray? Instead of giving into tears of sorrow, I'm now laughing happy, sloppy tears. Riding the good mood, I channel my strength through sarcasm. "I'd like to say, 'I'll drink to that,' but honestly, we all know I'll drink to just about anything. C'mon, ladies, let's go offend a whole bunch of people."

"Wait. We got you one, too, but it's just for your memory box. Plus, the tray. I saw you eyeing it."

I wipe a tear. "I love you, bitches."

"We know." Carrie yawns.

The girls change into their *TEAM TESS* shirts while I debate which of my new T-shirts to wear tonight. I decide the status shirt is most appropriate for the situation and switch my current top for the T-shirt.

The couch is strewn with cast-off halter and tube tops. I feel a twinge of anxiety, and my hands clench and twitch. I just want to fold the clothes. Is that so bad?

Instead, I lean over the table and blow out the evergreen candle. I wave the swirl of smoke drifting toward the ceiling. With a clink, I gather two empty beer bottles and reach for a plastic cup.

Rory slaps my hand. "I called the litter police and gave them the night off."

I nod. Good thing I resisted the shirts.

"Let's get ready to stumble!" Mel announces with a loud, extra-deep voice through cupped hands.

I yearn to clean the mess, but instead, I take a giant step forward and throw back my shoulders. I beam and place both hands on my hips. "Hold my dignity, please. I've got some sketchy shit to attend to."

Alexa links her arm through mine, and the rest of the girls follow suit. We create a circle as if we're about to perform a cheer and run out on a court or playing field.

"Now there's the Tess we would wear matching T-shirts in public for. Let's go!"

Chapter Fourteen

We break out of the group hug, and for the first time, I feel the void of Hannah who would've said something positive and poignant at this moment. "I miss Hannah. No, you know what, screw her. She chose the other team tonight." I only dare speak badly of her if she's not around. In truth, she rarely does anything wrong and admitted to feeling completely conflicted about attending the wedding. She offered many times to stay with me, but I wouldn't, couldn't, let her.

Leah turns toward Mel. "Speaking of Hannah…"

Alexa leans in and punches Leah's arm. "I don't believe we were."

Leah rubs her arm. "Geez, I only mentioned her because she asked me to share her roast."

"She doesn't get one—the traitor." I fake a snarl. "Plus, we are almost out the door." I point and hope to escape without another trip down embarrassing memory lane. I've had enough and am ready to make a physical move now. The apartment air feels oppressive, not that I imagine the bar will offer a cool breeze. I walk toward the door but feel a tug on the back of my shirt.

"Down, girl." Carrie laughs. "Let's hear it, Leah. Apparently, we have time."

I want to ask what she means, but I'm not quick enough.

Leah steps onto the table. "Actually, she wrote

several." Leah pulls a piece of paper out of the back pocket of her skintight, denim skirt.

Once the paper is flattened, I see it's the back of an order sheet from the restaurant where Leah works.

"Oh, Hannah went all Classic Celebrity Roast here." She simultaneously winces and giggles.

"Here goes. '*Tess and Adam go together like drunk and disorderly.*' "

A collective, pitiful laugh is heard from the couch where we've re-deposited ourselves.

" '*Tess doesn't just make mistakes; she sleeps with them.*' "

A longer laugh emits but still not at full-strength.

" '*Whenever Tess says she's just run into Adam, I always ask why she didn't shift into Reverse and back up over him.*' "

Groans fill the room.

"Lame," I yell through cupped hands.

" '*Tess has been called a bitch, but she's been called worse...like Adam's girlfriend.*' "

True laughter erupts.

"Better," I admit.

"Oh, this is good. Let's end with this one. '*Tess repeatedly taking back Adam is like taking a shower and then putting on the same dirty underwear.*' "

"Ha, so true," Rory says above everyone else's "Ews."

"Gross, yeah. Ha-ha," I reply to play along. Except, every time I went back to Adam, I felt like I slipped into my favorite, worn-soft pajamas. When I wasn't with him, I never felt truly relaxed. I'd give anything to have that cozy PJ feeling right now. I sniff and shake my head as if doing so could erase the thoughts running through my head.

"So, Hannah…" I say and glance around the room. Why won't any of these drunk girls break tonight? Usually, after a couple of drinks, they spill just about anything. Some of the most important information has been leaked courtesy of cocktails.

"No can do, Tess. We can't tell you what she's saying."

Leah walks past me toward the bathroom. "Or not saying."

"So, she is still texting?" I ask. "She must be at the reception by now." I feel my hands open and close fast Are they thanking their guests for coming? Taking family group photos? Being introduced as Mr. and Mrs. Powers? Ugh, I might puke for real this time. According to the covers of my numerous notebooks and journal entries, I was supposed to be Tess Powers. I hope Brittany keeps her own, stupid last name. She shouldn't get his. I feel like I just lost a round of kickball and no longer want to play, but I yearn to take my ball and go home.

Alexa shakes her head. "We told her to stop. No one has heard from Hannah in over an hour. Quit thinking about it." She scoots over and hugs me.

"I'm trying." I frown. "I'm sorry, but tonight is tough, Alexa. I want to joke and have fun, but it's challenging."

"Stop picturing the reception," Alexa says.

"I know I should, but I can't help it. The weird thing is, I just keep seeing her, not him. My mind probably won't let me. Stupid brain."

"Oh, Tess." She releases her embrace and takes both my twitchy hands in hers and squeezes. "How did we get here?"

"Booze and bad decisions?" I emit a choked laugh. I want to have fun, but my tears defy me.

"We call that the combo number one." Rory raises a pointer finger.

"What's the value meal?" Mel smirks.

"A booty call?" I ask.

Everyone laughs.

I pull my hands free from Alexa's, hoping I won't need the restraint any longer. I also need to wipe my eyeliner and probably start my makeup from scratch.

"Then what do you call an afternoon quickie?" Mel asks.

"An extra value meal." I crack up at my response and can't stop. "Wait, I've got another. Twice in one day?"

"Easy," Carrie yells. "A daily double."

"Oh, the smell of fries," Leah says.

"You mean the smell of acne," Alexa groans. "I couldn't go near anything greasy for years."

We all laugh and talk over each other about slushies, wieners, and double-deckers. Junior high-level humor always saves the day.

Eventually, Rory sighs and pulls out a compact mirror and lip gloss.

I'm amused watching her attempt to apply the pink frost neatly.

She licks her lips and snaps shut the mirror. "Good old fast food. It's always there for you. You know it's bad for your health but tastes just too good to resist. I've heard they add some highly addictive ingredient designed to keep you coming back for more."

"Like Adam." I nod.

"But fast food will never leave you for another." Mel points.

"Unlike Adam," I respond.

Leah returns from the bathroom in time to join in the fun. "And fast food can't cheat."

"Well, Adam only cheated with me," I say. "Not on me."

"Shut up," Carrie says.

"What?" I look around the room to gauge their puzzled reactions. "He's cheated on others with me, but he's never cheated on me while we were together. You know, officially."

Leah tosses a pillow. "Get out of here."

"What? I'm serious." I take in the stunned faces of my friends. My stomach drops. This is news to them. Is this why they don't think we belong together? No, I panic. "Wow, do all of you think he's cheated? I know for a fact he never did. And for the record, I never cheated on him either."

I shift in my seat. The girls avoid my gaze and fidget with their phones and jewelry.

Mel clears her throat. "No offense, Tess, but this news is kind of hard to believe."

My heart is racing, and I can't catch my breath. I need to move and jump to my feet. "Oh my God, you guys. Have you just assumed over all these years we were like that? That *I am*? You thought I'd let him use me and keep coming back for more?"

"Uh, yeah." Alexa turns to Carrie. "Right?"

Carrie shrugs. "I just thought, you know, he's a dog like every other guy."

A nervous-sounding giggle erupts. I don't know who started the trend, but soon they are all laughing.

"What's so funny?" I ask.

Leah cocks her head. "You have to admit, Tess, it's weird for us to think Adam never cheated."

The rest of the group nods.

"It's not weird. It's true," I say through gritted teeth. I pick up a pillow and punch it.

I want to understand their reaction, but I can't suppress my own. I clench my jaw to keep from speaking before thinking and turn my back on the girls. Heat creeps up my neck, a sign I'm mad even though I want to remain cool. I've put up with a lot from Adam but never would've tolerated cheating, and I certainly would not have taken him back. Okay, maybe when I was a younger teenager, I guess, but not in the recent, so-called adult years. Now I'm furious just thinking all my friends thought that's exactly what I had been doing all these years.

I turn to face my friends. I want my voice to sound neutral, but I can't prevent delivering a note of irritation. "I'm serious, you guys. Cheating would've been a deal-breaker. We weren't always good to each other, but we were always faithful. C'mon, why would I lie about that? Especially now. Please, believe me." I know I'm being loud, too loud, and don't care. I'm fuming and want them all to comprehend how serious I am and upset at the misconception. I can't stand still and pace the space between the coffee table and couch.

"Shit." Alexa takes a noisy swig from her beer.

"Damn, you're pissed, Tess." Carrie blinks several times. "You mush, I mean must, be telling the truth." She hiccups, as if on cue.

"Yeah, um I don't know why I always thought he cheated, but I can't think of an instance." Mel scrunches her face.

I imagine she, and the rest of the girls, are mentally searching the timeline of our lives for clues.

"If you're not lying, I feel terrible, but now have a million questions," Rory says.

I've been pacing the same four-foot patch of carpet and now stomp in place. "Fire away!" I grab the closest beer bottle from the table.

"Okay, then. What about our senior prom?" Mel asks.

I shake my head. "Nothing happened with Joel."

Leah throws back her head. "Ha! That's not what Joel told everyone."

Grinning, I roll my eyes and put down the warm beer I couldn't possibly stomach now. A chalky antacid would be welcome. "Believe me, I know what he said. Joel was nice enough to agree to be my date, so I did him a big favor by letting him say whatever he wanted afterward. We had an arrangement."

"Huh." Rory shakes her head. "I seem to recall seeing that in an eighties movie."

I drop my shoulders, and my face relaxes. "Yeah, I guess I never told you the story, Rory. I pulled it off for his sake. Hey, being gay was hard back then. Now, he's out and happy. The last I heard from him, he sounded like he's been getting more action than any of us." I grin. "No harm, no foul."

I smile to myself remembering the conversations Joel and I shared in the weeks before the dance. I truly believed Adam would change his mind and take me, despite his excuse of having to study for final exams. Joel sat behind me in math, and I loved the friendly banter we traded. I had shared my Adam dilemma, and

I felt like he sympathized.

One day he asked if he could call me with a proposition.

I was intrigued.

He called later to explain, and I instantly liked his idea. We got to attend prom with the understanding we both wished we were with someone else. Misery loves company, and because of this, I had an awesome time. I didn't have to worry about my date getting sloppy drunk, and as a bonus, Joel proved to be a great dancer.

He, in turn, bought himself more time to admit to his family he's more of a Ted than a Tess guy.

"Wow." Rory raises her eyebrows. "Bold move."

"Thank you." I curtsy.

"And later, we'll revisit how you kept that a secret all this time." Mel draws a wide invisible circle in the air. "For now, though, I need to know—are you certain he never cheated?"

"As certain as I can be." I lower my voice. "We've had a lot of late-night heart-to-hearts. I'm not naïve. I know he had plenty of opportunities through the years, but I believe him. Also, the last time we talked he had no reason to lie or hold back anything."

"Still." Alexa shrugs. "I can't shake all these thoughts now."

"Same," says Mel.

"Yeah, like how do you explain Adam's trip to the Cape the summer after his graduation?" Carrie points her finger like a pistol. "Not to be a bitch or anything, but I figure no holding back tonight, right?"

"Oh yeah." Alexa jumps to her feet. "Or better yet, our trip the following year for our graduation? How do you explain Nate?" She sing-songs this blast-from-the-past name.

If she's trying to irritate me, she's succeeding. Now my guard is up, and I know I sound defensive, but whatever. "Easily," I say and try to remain calm. "The fling with Nate—and that's all it was, just a little kissing—was all perfectly legit. Adam and I were not together in June. After the prom with Joel, I didn't speak to Adam again until the Fourth of July."

"You did more than just speak at Katie's second annual Red, White, and Blue party, I recall," Mel adds.

"That was a great party." Leah's voice trails off.

Carrie side-eyes Leah. "Is that where we first met Kelly B.?"

Heads turn to face Leah, who snaps back to attention and reddens.

She throws back her hair and turns. "You still haven't addressed Adam's trip."

"Fine, but you haven't addressed anything."

Rory claps her hands and lifts her chin. "Okay everyone, take mental notes, and let's direct the spotlight back on you, Tess."

"Okay, okay." I nod. "I might have led you all to believe everything was cool with me and Adam around the time of his graduation, but in truth, we were on a break."

"Like Ross and Rachel?" Alexa retreats to the couch.

"Exactly, Alexa. That time we were, in fact, just like Ross and Rachel. We both decided he should be officially unattached for the end of high school. Therefore, whatever he did that weekend after his graduation was his business, not mine."

Carrie cackles. "And I heard his business got

busy."

"Just remember, you also heard I rocked Joel's world, and now you know I'm not equipped."

"Hmm." Leah narrows her eyes.

"You must have asked him what happened during that weekend at some point?" Alexa cocks her head.

"Nope." I shake my head. "Breaks are breaks, and no questions are allowed." I hope to sound convincing, but the proclamation has never sat well. I've wanted to ask about other girls many times over the years, but nausea and dread prevented me.

"Well, I have one more question." Mel raises a pointer finger. "So, were you officially dating on the night he climbed through your window?"

I straighten my back and square my shoulders. "Of course, we were together again."

"All right. What was the date of that 'special night'?"

"I forget," I mutter.

"No, you don't." Mel shakes her finger in my face. "No one forgets."

I grab her finger and lower it. "Fine. July eighth"

The ensuing silence causes me to assume they are doing the mental math and figuring the dates don't add up. Believe me, I've used creative arithmetic, too. I fear they remember the unusually loud fight between me and Adam at Katie's first annual Red, White, and Blue party.

I exhale and rehearse my answer to the yet-unasked question I believe is on all their minds. "Yes, I was doing everything I could to keep him. He was leaving for college while I was staying behind, so of course, I was scared. Whatever. Go ahead and interpret however you'd like. It doesn't matter now anyway." I sputter the last sentence. I'd like to avoid the nuclear meltdown I sense bubbling inside my chest. "Nothing matters."

"Tess, I don't think anyone here means to upset you." Rory scans the room. "It's just, well, I think we're all having a hard time processing this revelation about you two being faithful. I personally have only witnessed the last ten years, and I just assumed you both cheated during college with all the break-ups and back and forths. I can only imagine what the other girls are thinking."

Alexa scratches her head. "I don't know what to think."

"I feel really bad, like sick-to-my-stomach bad." Leah clutches her middle.

"Yeah, me too," Carrie says.

I snort. "Join the club."

"Right." Alexa lowers her voice to an apologetic whisper. "I mean, this news kind of changes things."

"How?" I cross my arms over my chest. "How does this revelation have anything to do with him marrying Brittany? C'mon, look at the time. They've probably had their first dance as husband and wife by now."

"Maybe," Leah says.

"Shut up, Lee." Carrie smacks her arm.

"Mel?" Alexa asks through gritted teeth. "What about…"

Mel returns a glare at Alexa with eyebrow-raising then turns to me with a straight face.

"Tess." She places her hands on my shoulders. "You need to listen carefully. The girls and I need to talk privately right now. You'll have to trust us. I'm sorry to say I don't trust you though." She sighs. "Please lock yourself in the bathroom and turn on the fan. Can you do that?"

I narrow my eyes and scowl. "Why?"

"We need to discuss something. I promise once we figure it out, we'll tell you everything. Swear you won't try to listen. Just give us five minutes, tops." She holds up her hand, fingers splayed.

Alexa nods.

Mel sounds sober. Her mouth is set in a tight line. I know from experience not to mess with this version of her. I take a step back. "I could say so much about locking the guest of honor in her bathroom." I slink to my jail cell. "I'll go, but only to calm down for a minute."

"Thank you, Tess. I know this seems weird," Mel says.

After a quick pee and makeup check in the bathroom mirror, I do what anyone else would in this situation. I attempt to listen. Smooshing my ear against the door proves futile. Then I spy a quarter-inch gap between the door and the floor. I squat, hunch over, and twist my head, but I fall over. Once on the floor, it makes sense to just go flat. The cold tile feels nice. I know it's clean because I scrubbed every surface in the apartment this morning in a flurry of nerves. I dismissed the compulsion as a desire for everything to look nice for my so-called party. I'm especially grateful now for bleach and ammonia, but I curse the thick carpeting in the other room muffling my friends' voices. The voices in my head, however, are loud and clear. I wonder if I should lay it all on the line now and tell them about the not-exactly-a-proposal. But what good would confessing do? I could tell them my exclusive, inside knowledge that Adam and Brittany have never slept together. Yup, I'm still his only and him mine. I doubt my friends would even believe me, and if they did, sharing could only make them sad along with me.

Nausea rises as I realize, after tonight, I won't be his only. I roll to my side and into the fetal position. I'm not ready for this. All that tough talk was crap. I want this horrible feeling of rejection to magically disappear.

I picture Adam and Brittany at the head table, thanking guests and kissing at the prompt of clinking spoons to wineglasses. I can't do this. I want to stay on the floor. The floor is comforting. Ultimately, a gentle knock decides my fate.

"Warning, back away from the door. I'm about to open it, and I'm guessing you have your ear pressed against the other side."

Damn, these girls know me. Although, Mel is wrong—my feet are against the door. "I'm fine," I shout. I push myself to stand and straighten my clothes. I want her to be honest and tell me everything just discussed. If I look messy, I know she will try to protect me by sugar-coating whatever just transpired. I take a deep breath and slowly twist the doorknob. The lock pops with a loud click.

Her shoulders are slumped and the corners of her mouth downturned. "This might seem petty, probably even two-faced, but we were wrong. Please forgive us."

As I process this apology, I wonder if Mel is insinuating more than I comprehend through my foggy head. I struggle to decipher what she could mean but give up. "I don't understand."

She shakes her head. "I wouldn't expect you to. Let me back up."

She places a hand on my right shoulder and leads me back into the main room where the rest of my friends wait with hangdog expressions.

"See, we let you Adam-bash all you wanted, which I think is okay. He's been yours to bash. We were supposed to support you and chime in with our comments, too, but we crossed the line to ridicule."

"But," adds Rory. "We did so under pretenses. Not that I'm making excuses."

"No." Alexa straightens her spine. "We're offering explanations with apologies, not excuses. There is a big difference."

"Okay." I roll my eyes. "This all sounds terrific, but I'm still a little fuzzy. Why the sudden intervention?"

Mel steps back and addresses the room. "We all just assumed you both cheated over the years. More importantly, we believed he cheated and treated you badly. We took the assumption as a license to hate on him. Or at least, I did. I must add here, my recent man situation might have me jaded. Just saying."

"I agree." Rory nods. "The truth is, I think we all liked you and Adam together, and his marrying Brittany has hurt us, too. We found believing you two weren't good for each other easier than feeling the pain. Making fun of him and of you as a couple helped us accept the reality and support you tonight."

I recall now all the positive and wonderful times with Adam and wonder if I shared enough of those good times with my friends. Did I only complain about the bad? Sure, in the early years I drove them crazy with gushing about how great I thought he was. But as adults, did I let them know how great he truly turned out? I know he's their friend, too, but I'm certain they are unaware of his most admirable qualities.

Adam is quite humble, and some of his greatest achievements have been swept under the rug at his request. I only discovered his promotions in passing from colleagues because he would never brag. Of the accomplishments I have been privy to in the past, he always asked me to keep them private. To this day, my friends don't know, and I doubt his do either, that he was accepted to three prestigious universities, with two offering scholarships. They were all far from home, and he ultimately chose Stonehill to remain closer to Darcy and not place a travel burden on his family. He passed up studying abroad while all his buddies went to underage drink their way through Europe. He lied about having to retake a class when in fact he graduated with extra credits and a 3.8 GPA. The selfless, wonderful guy who I love—yes, I do—deserves better. I don't regret keeping his secrets and respecting his privacy, but I wish my friends understood.

They know all about the gifts Adam gave me over the years, but they don't know the numerous times he supported me with tough decisions. His advice was not only helpful but well thought out and sincere. He never hesitated to answer a late-night call when I struggled with a school, work, or family issue. I have always appreciated his encouragement, but did I ever let the girls know I valued his opinion?

The revelation of us never cheating seems to resonate with them, and I hope they can now understand what a terrible loss I am experiencing. Then again, maybe Brittany tells her friends all the wonderful things Adam does. Maybe he really did marry the right girl. Either way, she's at her reception, and I'm here, facing the inquisition of my friends who are waiting for me to accept their apology for thinking the worst of Adam.

"I see." I nod. "And now you want me to say I understand. Well, I do, and I'm partly to blame for you all believing we were unfaithful to each other. However, now you sound like you've changed your stance. I appreciate your honesty, but the revelation doesn't change anything about tonight. Unless you want to just make this a tear-fest from here on in, or call it quits."

Mel steps forward. "No, there's more, but again, you'll have to believe that right at this moment we know what's best." Mel clasps our hands. "I know it's asking a lot, and you've been so strong already, but please just trust us once more. After, you're free to call all the shots."

The others mutter agreements.

I search the room to lock gazes with one of them in hopes of gathering more info, but no heads rise. I'm left to continue negotiating with my captor. "You are pushing my limits of trust, Mel."

Mel takes a deep, yoga-type inhale. "I know. You've been a trouper, and we've been vague. I received information, but I'm not entirely sure the source is reliable. We all want to protect you, but after discussing, and in light of recent developments, we agree you should make your own decisions once we get to the Phoenix. Clearly, you've made better ones than we've given you credit for. For now, though, you need to come with us. And sorry, no questions allowed."

I turn to confront the rest of the group. "Girls, stop avoiding me and making Mel do this alone. Give me a sign I should still go. I want to trust you, but you've got to give me some assurance."

They all nod, and a few offer weak smiles.

Rory mutters, "Yes."

Carrie nods, too, but she looks like she might barf.

Finally, Leah breaks from the group and silently pulls me into a hug.

I feel like I'm receiving a hug from a great-aunt at a wake. Like she is comforting herself more than me, but she doesn't know what else to do. I pull out of the awkward embrace and force a tight-lipped smile of appreciation. "I surrender." I lift my hands in the air. "What choice do I have?"

Chapter Fifteen

Just as I'm about to place my hand on the doorknob, releasing us into the night, I freeze. My limbs paralyze while my mind races. Snippets of memories flash like a slideshow in my mind. Nausea builds, and a familiar burning behind my eyes returns.

I spin to face my friends lined up behind me. "Maybe we should go somewhere other than the Phoenix." I deliver a hint of unintentional whining.

Leah gasps and throws a hand over her heart. "What? Are you suggesting other bars might exist in the Commonwealth of Massachusetts?"

"I think this might not be the best night to broaden our horizons," Mel enunciates.

I assume she wants to ensure we all hear. Or do I detect the possibility of a hidden message?

Nervous now, I wonder if a surprise awaits me at the Phoenix and whether I should be excited or scared. Why is she urging us to go there? I force my body to move and grab Mel's elbow, pulling her close. I hope she'll confide or confess. "What are you hiding, Mel?"

"Nothing." She shakes loose. "Well, that's not exactly true…maybe you should…"

Unfortunately, I am denied the revelation.

Carrie sneaks from behind and clamps a hand over Mel's mouth.

With her hand still on Mel, Carrie twists her head.

"Why don't you want to go to the Phoenix, Tess?"

I swirl my hands around my head. "It's just full of memories. You know, Tess and Adam memories. Good, bad, and all the in-betweens. All these old scenes keep rushing at me." I can't hide the sadness in my voice. I sound like an eight-year-old negotiating a later bedtime. I dab at my eyes, as if forcing in the tears.

Rory slips on a cropped denim jacket and re-straps her silver sandals. "My mind is racing, too, but soon we'll kill a few more brain cells and should be on the dance floor boogying away our cares. Anyway, it's safe for you to lose your shit in the Phoenix. Think about facts for a second. Most importantly, Laurie won't call the cops on us."

"True that," Carrie says. "She would have been justified having our asses hauled out plenty of nights in the past."

"Oh my God. Remember the catfight between you and Leah?" Rory asks Carrie.

"Do we?" Leah laughs. "Each year, we mark the anniversary with a commemorative dinner."

"Hey, now! It took months for my hair to grow back." Carrie touches her scalp and cringes.

Leah snorts. "Lighten up. It was a weave—and a bad one. You should thank me for doing you a favor."

"You want a piece of me, shorty?" Carrie raises her fists.

The group gasps, but then they hug.

I groan and walk out of my apartment and down the stairwell. The clip-clop of high heels and wedges echoes like a herd of elephants.

As they walk, Leah keeps her arm around Carrie. "See, we're good. We're like Tess and Adam."

"God, I hope you two don't do what Adam and I do after a fight. Gross." I swing from a laugh to a choking sniff. "Of course, I mean what we used to do." The image of us in bed stops me in my tracks. One of the girls bumps into me from behind. I don't bother looking to see who or apologize.

Mel swoops to my side. She grabs my arm and steers me toward the sidewalk. "No tears. Our ride-share is here. If you can't walk, I'll carry you, but it's now or never. You shouldn't risk going anywhere else tonight, and you know it. Plus, there's the whole rising from the ashes metaphor that must not be ignored. So, the Phoenix it is."

Ten minutes later, I approach the dive that has been my second home since I scored my first fake ID. None of us could celebrate our twenty-first birthdays here for obvious reasons, but this has been our go-to for everything else. Normally, I would risk seeing Adam or his friends here on a Saturday night. Sometimes, I look for said trouble, but tonight we're safe.

That crowd is dancing at Crystal Banquets now. Maybe they're sipping champagne and sampling the dessert table. I'm sure they hold little, white cocktail napkins printed with the bride's and groom's names and today's date in Brittany's signature color—fuchsia. Darcy thought it was a very sophisticated choice and told me the bridesmaid dresses were, "Short, super-shiny, and have no arms." I oohed in agreement with Darcy at the time and silently judged Brittany. Now the thought of strapless, hot-pink taffeta has me wiping tears with my knuckles, not making comparisons to hookers. I hesitate short of the entrance.

Mel leans in close. "Remember, sometimes the

grass is greener on the other side because it's fake."

"I like that one." I feel slightly better. I want to be okay, but I know by the clock illuminated on my phone the marriage is a done deal. The ceremony ended hours ago. Adam and Brittany are husband and wife. I nod and squeeze her arm to show my sincerity.

Mel purses her lips. "I know you're trying, and who knows what will happen. So if it all gets to be too much, just say the word, and I'll get you out."

"Thank you," I mutter. Mel keeps a hand on my back. I bet she's worried. Normally, I'm a loose cannon. Tonight, I'm sure to be a powder keg.

I take a deep breath of the warm night air. I roll my head, shuffle my feet, and shake my arms like I'm about to enter the ring to face the reigning champ. "Let's do this." I'm not as drunk as I should be, considering the amount I've consumed, but just enough to believe entering the bar is now a good idea.

We strut into the noisy, half-filled bar.

The floor is sticky and the air stale. Some things never change, and I'm thankful for the familiarity. I smile and relax my shoulders.

Laurie greets us, carrying a tray laden with cinnamon shots.

One of the girls must have texted her to alert our arrival. We form a sloppy circle around her.

She passes out the tiny glasses and raises her own.

She rarely drinks while working and seldom makes exceptions. I don't know whether to consider myself honored or pitied.

"To Tess, tough as nails and hot as hell. Don't worry, sweetie, you'll be just fine!" She throws back the shot and blows a kiss. Pivoting on her heels, she returns to her spot behind the bar, pouring drafts and mixing drinks with bottom shelf liquor.

We toss back our shots and fist pump in unison. Our circle gains a few stares and pointed fingers.

A random girl scans us head-to-toe. She leans over and speaks directly in another girl's ear.

With both hands, Carrie flips off the girl.

Classy and effective.

As if on cue, the band returns from a break. The local group of misfits occasionally play their own songs, but they know the crowd will revolt unless they play classic late 1990s tunes. They ascend the makeshift stage. The twang and screech of their warm-up cuts our chatter.

Laurie pours draft beers into mismatched pint glasses and lines them on the side of the bar closest to the area we use as a dance floor.

We're predictable. Thankfully, the band has assessed their crowd and opens with an old favorite which gets us out on the floor and singing along.

I pick up a glass, ignore the sticky exterior, and welcome the refreshing coolness sliding down my parched throat. I'm sure I'll have no voice tomorrow, but I refuse to let the inevitable result stop me. I cup my hands around my mouth. "Girls! Assume your positions."

As usual, our group repels as many people off the floor as we welcome on. I spy some familiar faces who offer sympathetic looks or touch my arm. I appreciate it, but now I just want to sing at the top of my lungs and stomp around until my head spins and my feet throb. This is my therapy, and the girls are my support group. We stay together for two songs.

"I see someone at the bar I need to talk with. I'll meet you out on the floor in a bit." Mel slinks away.

"Yeah, um. Rory and I are going to the ladies' room." Alexa grabs Rory's elbow.

I shrug and lead Leah and Carrie to the perimeter of the crowd near four, semi-familiar-looking guys. I half dance, half shout along with the songs.

Eventually, Carrie gets closer to one of the guys, and they worm their way toward the stage together.

"You go, girl," I yell.

The other three guys follow the couple. They don't look back.

I shrug and continue to dance. After a couple of songs, I'm out of breath and sweaty. I grab Leah's hand and lead her to the side of the bar where our beers have been magically replaced with plastic cups of water. *God bless, Laurie.* I chug and turn to see if Leah wants to sit for a minute or head back to jump and shout. One of her favorite songs is playing, so it's odd for her not to be dancing.

She's no longer close but sitting on a stool and staring at her phone.

I call her name repeatedly, but she doesn't respond. I pick up on a weird vibe. I tap her shoulder but not gently.

Leah widens her eyes and tightens her lips into a straight line.

I wonder if she's literally biting her tongue. "What is so important on your phone?"

She slides her hand down and reveals a familiar design.

The phone is mine. I discreetly pat my back pocket and discover it flat. I clench my hands and panic about what messages I missed.

She winces. "You left this on the bar, and it looks like it's been going berserk for the last twenty minutes." She scans the room and opens her palm.

I feel dirty accepting the phone, but I can't wait to investigate.

Alexa and Mel fly over but stop just short of reaching me. They clutch their phones to their chests. "Don't! Don't look at your phone yet."

"Listen to us," Mel says. "We need to talk before you do anything."

"What do you mean do something? What would I do? I don't have any idea what you're talking about." I stomp. "Enough of these vague references and trust me bullshit. I have been so patient. Somebody, please clue me in. You promised you'd let me know." I continue tapping the incorrect four-digit code with my fumbling, sweaty fingers.

"We'll tell you everything. Just promise not to look at your phone." Mel presses her palms together and tucks them under her chin. "We can explain better than any cryptic message you're probably receiving. Please, Tess? The texts will only confuse you more."

I raise my phone and make a show of sliding it into my back pocket. I failed to unlock it and must wait for the probation period to expire before attempting again. "Happy now?" I lean closer to Mel.

"It's for the best; trust me." She grips my forearm. "Listen. I know, just this one last time, please. You know I would never do anything to hurt you."

"I'm seriously beginning to question that promise." Above the noise of the bar, I can still hear pinging and dinging. My butt vibrates from my own phone's notifications, but I resist looking. What's the point? I can't read the full message anyway, only the notification on the locked screen.

The girls all look at each other and back at their phones with wide eyes and gasps.

I hear more buzzing and beeping and feel my temperature skyrocketing. I pull my hair away from my sweaty neck, but I find no relief.

They scroll, swipe, and type with lightning speed while yelling and repeating a collective mantra. "No f-ing way!"

"Are they from Hannah? At least tell me that much." I shake Mel by the shoulders.

Her head bobs loosely.

They nod but don't make eye contact. Everyone, except Carrie, now stands before me looking at their phones, gasping and swearing.

"What could she possibly say that I don't already know?" I throw my hands above my head. "Was the cake missing a tier, or was the champagne not the perfect shade of trashy pink? Oh, no wait. Something must have gone awry with the garter toss. Spare me the details." I motion for Laurie to hit me up with another drink. Anything will do at this point.

Laurie rolls her eyes but then turns to the tap.

"Nope." Rory shakes her head.

"This is cruel. I want to tell her," Alexa says.

"Something happened," Leah mutters. "Or, to be technical, didn't happen."

I nod and lean in, trying to hear every word over the bar noise. I'm fed up with this charade. I played nice all night, but I have my limits. I lunge for Mel's phone.

She pulls her arm back just in time. "I'm sorry. You have every right to be pissed. I just don't know yet what to tell you. We don't have any details. I promise you we'll explain once we learn the whole story."

Rory scrolls through messages and widens her eyes every few seconds. "Yeah, I'm not exactly clear, but I think what we thought might have happened actually did."

Leah knits her eyebrows. "Huh?"

Alexa looks up from her phone. "Madeline was there and thinks it's true. I do, too."

"Did you all see the photo from Tyler?" Rory asks.

"Yup." Leah stuffs her phone in her back pocket. "So, what happens now?"

"I don't know." Rory shrugs. "Be ready for anything, I guess."

Laurie passes a beer through the crowd.

Mel grabs the overflowing glass and extends her arm. "Here, Tess. I think you'll need this." She shakes foam from her hand.

I'm sick of this bizarre exchange. I snatch the beer and resist inhaling it. "Never mind. It's too late now."

"Or is it?" Alexa tilts her head toward the door.

I side-eye her then turn my gaze at the bar's entrance. I slap my hand over my gaping mouth to stifle the gasp.

Adam walks through the doorway.

Chapter Sixteen

He's still wearing his tuxedo…partially. His shirt is untucked, open-collared, and bow-tieless. At one point today, he probably looked amazing. Now, not so much. But he's here. Adam is in the Phoenix—alone.

I immediately squint at his left hand. I don't even hide my blatant stare. I do not see a ring. I gasp again. I can't tell if he's mad, sad, drunk, or all three.

But as his gaze meets mine, his face softens.

I relax mine. I only care that he is here. I feel my heart pound, and beads of sweat form. I try to hide my smile. I don't even know if I have anything to smile about yet, but I can't stop grinning now. I can't help but wonder if my earlier wish got granted, or if this is just a dream, and Brittany will waltz in the door any second.

I believe his being here means something. I hope something good. Then again, I need to be the strongest I've ever been in case it is not. Breaking down in front of the girls is one thing, and I've had enough for tonight. I straighten my spine and roll my shoulders. My untouched beer is removed from my hands. I feel like I'm about to take a test, and though prepared, I must now recall all I know in my head and my heart.

Adam shuffles closer.

My previously paralyzed legs come to life and inch toward him. At the same time, I sense my friends retreating. I know they wouldn't do so unless they were

231

certain I'd be okay. And I will. I've needed them all night, but I have to face Adam alone now. I got what I wanted. I think. At least that's what I sense right now. All I wanted was for him to want me. Now, face to face, I know before he speaks, but I still need to hear him say the words.

He opens his mouth but doesn't speak.

I swallow hard. My ears ring, and my head buzzes.

He blinks rapidly.

All the thoughts in my head fight to escape from my mouth before I have a chance to organize them. The obvious flees first. "What are you doing here?"

He runs his hands through his hair. "Looking for you, of course."

"But, uh, Brittany." I don't know how to ask him what happened and blurt the remainder of my fragmented thoughts. "The wedding. You're here. What? You are supposed to be at your wedding. What happened? Her?"

His eyes widen. "Wow. No one told you yet?"

My legs wobble. "Told me what?"

Adam shoves both hands in his tuxedo pockets. He shuffles and clears his throat. "I couldn't go through with it. I don't know how it ever got this far. I knew this morning. No, I've known all along. I just didn't know how or when to stop the charade. I'm a total wimp. Last night's phone call was a pathetic attempt to convince you to beg me to call it off. I couldn't even do that right. I'm sorry."

Shit. If only I'd read between the lines, maybe I could have spared us all. Angry at myself for missing the opportunity, I ball my hands into tight fists at my sides and focus on figuring out what happened. "But, so…when did you, um, deliver the news? At the altar? I want to know, but you don't have to tell me."

"Yes, I do, Tess. I owe you. I owe you more than an explanation, but I'll start with the story." He shuffles his feet. "God only knows what version is floating around the bar now."

"Okay," I practically whisper.

Adam moves closer.

I desperately want to reach out and touch him, but I clasp my hands together. The sharp pain from my nails digging into my knuckles is sobering.

He visibly inhales and exhales. "I don't have an answer for how or why I got dressed and went to the church. I guess because I knew by the time I clipped on my tie she'd already be waiting."

"Hold up." I point to my own throat. "Did you say clip-on tie?"

"Only you would pick up on that detail. Yeah, I got one say on wedding arrangements, and I chose clip-ons for the guys. Geez, I'm having a moment here."

I hold up my hand. "Sorry. Please continue."

"Yeah, so I was supposed to go right to the altar from a side entrance, but I had stayed in the parking lot after my parents went inside. I texted Ryan."

—*Dude, can you come out here?*—

—*Sure.*—

A minute later, he was outside with me.

"What's up?" Ryan said as he approached.

I just kept my head down and shook it side to side.

"Yeah," he said. "I kinda figured. What can I do?"

"I'm gonna go find Brittany. Can you tell my dad?"

"I got you, Bro." Ryan patted my shoulder and

sauntered back into the church.

I guess he must have told my parents, and then the word spread. I snuck into the bride's room, which is actually just where they keep the robes and collection baskets. Anyway, Brittany wasn't in there yet, but the organist was playing the music that was supposed to tell her to get ready. At the rehearsal the other night, she told me that's when I was supposed to come out to the altar. She eventually walked into the bride's room with her cousin carrying the back of her dress. When she saw me, she didn't look surprised, more like mad.

"Hey, you're not supposed to be in here," her cousin said.

"Drop the train, Claire," Brittany snapped. "It doesn't matter anymore."

"Oh, shit. You want me to stay?"

Brittany shook her head.

"I told you I had a bad feeling about this one, Brit." Claire turned to me and pointed her finger in my face. "You're an ass," she snarled.

I hung my head while she hugged Brittany and whispered terrible things. When we were alone, I closed the door and rehearsed my so-called-sensitive speech, but she beat me to it.

"Go ahead and say it."

"You know?" My voice cracked.

"Of course, I know, but I still want to hear you say it." She crossed her arms and scowled. "I don't care if I sound cruel. Don't be a coward now."

"You're not being cruel. I am. I was cruel not to speak up. You deserve the truth."

"I deserved the truth yesterday."

Adam averts his gaze now in the bar and sniffs.

I know this is his way of composing himself to continue.

"I searched for the right words but blanked. I just stood there, looking stupid. I knew no way to make saying I couldn't marry her sound kind. Thankfully, she had helped soften the blow."

She sighed. "If we're being honest, though, then I knew the truth yesterday and the day before, and so on."

"I'm sorry," I told her. It was all I could say.

"Not sorry enough," she said.

"Being sorry and feeling guilty are not reasons to get married. You know…"

"Just go," she yelled.

I was afraid everyone in the church would hear.

"Just go to Tess. She's probably waiting outside behind a bush anyway."

"It's not like that, Brittany. Really. It's just, c'mon. This isn't right, you know that."

"Well, I wanted it to be, but you'll never get over Tess."

"You're right. I won't."

With dry eyes and pursed lips, she turned and flung open the door. Her mother, cousin, and the rest of the bridesmaids rushed in and ran to her side. They looked over their shoulders and shot me dirty looks.

"Whatever," she spat. "I can do better anyway." Her dress caught as she had tried to slam the door.

"I didn't know what to do, so I just waited a few minutes hoping everyone left and walked to the parking lot. I found Ryan listening to the radio in his parents' car. Not knowing what else to do, his parents left with mine to wait for me at our house. I never made it back.

Ryan and I drove around in silence for hours."

"Oh, Adam," I say. Even though I am relieved, I hate to think of him in pain. My chest is tight, but a welcome lightness enters my limbs I haven't experienced in months.

Adam moves closer, or I move closer to him. I'm not sure how, but we're only inches apart now.

"It's always been you, Tess." He extends a hand.

Placing my own in his, I feel the electricity of our first touch when I was fourteen return. A sense of hope eases my pulse. I hear the faint jingle of my charm bracelet. I forgot I was still wearing it and lift my wrist.

Adam reaches his other hand and touches it gently and smiles.

I lean into his chest and wrap my arms around his neck. "It's always been us," I whisper.

We linger in the embrace for a moment, then he pulls back so only our foreheads touch.

Despite the growing crowd, the intimacy I feel erases any hesitancy.

"I don't know what happens next, Tess, but I know whatever it is, I want us to be together. No more back and forth bullshit."

From behind my eyes the threat of tears burn, and I know my lips are visibly quivering. "Me, too," I eke out. I don't care if I cry now, these tears are welcome.

Adam lifts me off the ground by my waist until we are face to face. He grins and leans in for a kiss.

This is no public peck on the lips, but a long kiss—the kind I missed. His grasp feels both reassuring and like he's holding on for dear life. After the kiss, I bury my head into his neck and tighten my hold. Breathing in his familiar scent conjures good memories and steels my resolve. I want him to know nothing else matters anymore, and I won't ever let him go again.

Adam lowers me onto unsteady feet.

Reality strikes as I remember I am not alone with Adam but surrounded by people in a dive bar. This is the opposite of alone. Privacy will have to wait. I pull back and place a hand discreetly, but firmly, in his.

The crowded bar erupts into claps, shouts, and wolf whistles.

We're surrounded by my friends, and his have joined now, too. Other wedding guests have slipped in. Some I don't recognize, but I guess from their attire that the Phoenix wasn't their intended destination when they chose the flowery sundresses and lightweight, summer suits. I return smiles and mouth thank-yous before I finally spot Hannah standing next to Ryan.

She looks down to conceal a knowing smile, but she offers a thumbs-up.

We'll have a deep discussion later. I make a heart with my hands, place it over my heart, then hold it out toward her.

Ryan raises his beer in salute.

I scan the room for friends to thank. Everyone I love is here. Even Hunter is visible from his safe distance at the bar.

I make eye contact and offer a smile to let him know I'm glad he's here for Alexa. I appreciate the risk he takes being seen with her and expressing solidarity. It's no longer us versus them—like boys on one side, girls on the other at a junior high dance. They're all here for us. We're Team Tess and Adam. I'll have to order new shirts. My giddy smile morphs into a nervous giggle.

Adam shakes his head and laughs along. Slow at first, his chuckle builds to a full howl. His brown eyes are rimmed with red, but he flashes his wide smile and embarrassed-everyone-is-looking-at-us blush.

He finally looks like my Adam.

This is crazy. Yet it's fitting for us. I release a sigh, then I see my friends approaching. I should have known they would need to have their say.

Mel approaches first. She moves in and points a finger close to Adam's face. "You realize if either of you—and I mean you, Adam—changes your mind again, the homicide the girls and I commit will be justifiable?"

"Deal." Adam extends a hand.

Mel lowers her finger and shakes.

"And you!" She turns and punches my arm. "You have to keep your word about the dresses and the shower exceptions."

I nod and pump her hand.

Mel spins, wiggles her butt, and disappears into the crowd.

"Next!" Adam says.

Hannah steps in.

She's still wearing her dress, but her hair is a mess, and she's barefoot. She's also smiling like a lunatic and swaying.

She places a hand on Adam's upper arm. "Can I tell her?"

I detect a devious glint in her eyes. Or is it the booze?

He laughs. "Go ahead, Hannah. I couldn't stop you anyway, and I guess it's okay now."

Hannah giggles. "Darcy was in the back of the

church with the bridesmaids, fidgeting while she waited to drop the rose petals. When the organist stopped playing, everyone started whispering. Darcy, though, was not quiet. 'Where's Tess?' she asked."

"Oh my God!" I slap my right hand over my open mouth. I am quite familiar with Darcy's lack of volume control and can hear her sweet voice in my head.

Hannah relates how Adam's aunt jumped out of her pew and rushed to Darcy. She knelt and spoke to her quietly, but it did not appear Darcy got the message. "Everyone could see her turning around and searching the church." Hannah shakes her head. "She was so adorable, but probably extremely confused."

I tilt my face toward Adam. "You'll have some explaining to do later."

He gazes down and winks. "You mean we both will."

Hannah kisses my cheek and retreats to Ryan's side.

Ryan wraps his free arm around Hannah's shoulders and raises his beer toward me and Adam. He sets down the glass and, in a swift motion, unclips his bowtie and chucks it over his shoulder.

I take in the ever-growing crowd surrounding us and am overwhelmed. "I think I misspoke earlier." I turn from Adam to face my now, even larger group of friends, gathered before us. "This is my circus. You are my monkeys."

"We know," Alexa groans. Her wide smile betrays her tough act. Until now, she's been watching from a distance with crossed arms.

"Always the skeptic." I stretch my arms and make a puppy-dog expression.

She rolls her eyes, smirks, and crashes into my embrace.

"Break it up, Ringleader. It's time to celebrate." Adam calls Laurie for a round of shots and whistles the circus theme.

Alexa steps back.

Leah bursts through the crowd. She attacks me with a hug. She is sweaty from dancing.

"I knew it! I never doubted for a second." Her voice is raspy.

I put both hands on my hips and narrow my eyes.

Leah throws her arms in the air. "Okay, maybe for a second."

Carrie approaches and places an arm around Leah's shoulder. "Enough, Lee. Give them their night. The next intervention belongs to you."

Leah rolls her eyes and groans.

Carrie waves and pulls Leah back into the crowd.

Alexa gives a thumbs-up and follows Carrie and Leah.

Rory is the only friend remaining. She hesitates a moment, and then she slowly sidles over to where I stand beside Adam. "This is it, right?"

"What?" I'm honestly baffled.

Rory shakes her head. "The end? Happily-ever-after and all that crap?"

"Oh!" I slap my forehead and turn to Adam. "Well, um…"

Adam pulls me close to his side and rests his chin on top of my head. "Happily-ever-after—hell, yes. The end? Not by a long-shot."

A word about the author...

As the mother of three daughters, Ally finds creating drama for her characters an escape from the real drama in her own home. Originally from Boston, she now lives with her husband and family outside of Chicago.

Blog http://allyhayes.blogspot.com

Other titles by this author

Reality Re-Do
Secret Admirer

CPSIA information can be obtained
at www.ICGtesting.com
Printed in the USA
BVHW050428250921
617540BV00011B/587